Dark Harvest

William Malmborg

Saturday, September 15, 2012

Scott

Evidence of the drought that had plagued much of the country was all around Scott as he guided his car south along the rural Illinois road, the brown wilted cornstalks looking like something one would see creating the walls of a maze in a pumpkin patch as Halloween neared rather than a farm field in mid September.

Silent speculation on the economy and what the effects of this would be started to unfold, but then slipped away as a sign appeared.

Narrow Creek – 5 Miles

He glanced at the dashboard clock.

9:32.

Another five minutes and he would be entering the town, one that fell perfectly within the timeframe he had established.

And if they have a diner called something Café . . .

He didn't finish the thought, his mind not wanting to drum up hope once again that he had found it, only to have it ripped away. Nope. This time around he was going to wait and see; he was going to wait and --

The excitement arrived anyway, as did a sense that today things would be different. This time he would pull into town and see a diner on the main road, one with a name that ended in Café, and know without a doubt that this was where they had stopped to eat.

Then what?

He had asked himself this many times during the last two weeks, yet never really followed through with a solid answer.

Now was no different.

Too much depended on whether or not people remembered them, and, if so, what information they could provide. After that, he would have to make a decision on what to do with the information. Most would say bring it to the police. He, however, had lost confidence in their ability to handle something like this, especially after they had ignored what he had thought was a pretty solid rationalization of possible starting points for an investigation.

But maybe things will be different once you give them a verified starting point?

He considered this for a minute, but then came to the conclusion that without a body the police really didn't know what to do. They also didn't seem that keen on prioritizing missing adults.

Up ahead a small bridge appeared.

Like the withered cornstalks, the lack of water below in what had obviously been a decent sized creek at one point was evidence of the ongoing drought, one that a professor had actually told his class was quite possibility a result of the tsunami that had struck Japan back in March of 2011.

'So, not global warning as the liberal media would have us believe?' a fellow student had voiced. This in turn had sparked a debate, which prevented the professor from being able to explain just how the tsunami may have caused the drought.

Scott shook his head at the memory and then returned his focus to the task at hand, the appearance of the town up ahead causing his heart to speed up a bit.

Just a few more minutes and you'll know.
And if this is another strike out?

He had no answer, and, as it turned out, one was not needed. At least it didn't seem like it, not with a place called Carol's Café appearing seconds after he entered the small downtown area of Narrow Creek.

* * *

"Good morning," a cheery young voice echoed as he entered the diner. "Feel free to grab a seat anywhere you like and I'll be with you in a jiffy."

"Thanks," Scott replied and started scanning the place. Though not a boxcar diner, it had the layout of one in the front, booths on one side, counter on the other, a narrow aisle for walking between. Beyond the counter, things opened up allowing for diners to sit at tables in the large square area, all while booths continued to wrap along the wall.

Red cushioned booths.

Same as in the picture.

A sense of accomplishment started to build, one that grew even more as he took a seat and saw two small rectangular menus waiting in the back wire rack of the salt, pepper, and napkin stand.

"Coffee?"

He turned at the voice and saw a young lady looking down at him, coffee pot in hand, a beautiful smile on her face.

"Yes, please," he said, eyes drawn to the nametag that was being thrust forward by a nice, perfectly sized well-rounded boob. *Sophia.* "And some cream," he quickly added while she was filling the mug.

"You bet. Be right back."

He gave a *thank you* grin to her, which she did not see, and then pulled out the picture he had downloaded and printed from Facebook. In it sat Holly, a protesting smile on her face. Near the bottom right corner of the photo, her hand rested upon a menu.

Though it wasn't necessary given his confidence that he was in the right place, he took a second menu from the wire sleeve and set it across from him so that it was positioned identically to the one in the photo. Sure enough, it matched, only this time a casually placed hand wasn't covering part of the name printed along the top.

"Here you are," Sophia said while setting down the small cup of chilled cream. "Are you waiting on someone?"

"What?" he asked and then realized she was looking at the second menu. "Oops, no. Just seeing if this matched my photo." He held it up so she could see. "What do you think; does it look like she could have been sitting across from me?"

"Um . . . well, yes it does," Sophia said, a quizzical sound present in her voice. "Is this like a game or something?"

"I wish," Scott said. "Her name is Holly and she actually went missing two weeks ago. This is the last known photo taken of her. Were you working two weeks ago Saturday morning?"

"Yeah, every Saturday." Her voice took on that familiar somber tone that everyone always tries to display when presented with such information. "But I see so many people . . ." she gave a hopeless jester.

"Well, she was here looking for scarecrows," Scott said.
"Scarecrows?"

"Yeah, for a photo project." He waited a second. "Does that ring a bell?"

Sophia slowly shook her head. "Not really, but . . ." she looked over her shoulder toward the front of the diner ". . .

let me go ask my aunt."

"Okay."

She turned to head toward the register where an older lady was ringing up a customer, but then stopped and said, "Oh, want me to take your order really quick so that they can get started on it?"

"Um . . . let me look a bit," he said and held up a menu. A part of him wanted to simply find out if Holly and Ethan had been pointed in a specific direction and follow it. Another, however, knew his body needed food, especially after the depression induced weight loss he had suffered this summer, and decided to have a quick breakfast.

"Okay."

He opened the menu, a rumble from his stomach telling him he had made the right decision and started scanning the different meal suggestions.

Sophia returned a few seconds later.

"My aunt remembers them, but wasn't really able to help much."

"Shoot." *But at least they were here.* "Do you know of any farms in the area that would have some scarecrows?"

She shook her head, but then said, "I've seen them in the distance when driving though, so there are some out there. You might want to ask some of those folk if they remember your friends stopping by or something." She tapped her pen against her cheek a few times while thinking and, for a moment, he thought she might come up with something better, but then, "Yeah, that's all I can really think to do. Sorry."

"That's okay," he said. "You've helped me out quite a bit."

She smiled. "Really?"

Well, no, not really, the cynical part of his mind said.

"Yeah. Just knowing they were here is great because it finally gives me a starting point."

"Oh, I didn't think of that." She started tapping the pen again, only this time on her order pad. "Um . . . you still want to order something?"

"Yes," he said. "The two egg special with potatoes, bacon and pancakes, scrambled."

"Okay, hash browns or home fries for the potatoes?"

"Oh, how about hash browns."

"And any juice?"

He thought about that for a second. "Um, yeah, some orange juice."

"Great, I'll be back with that in a jiffy."

"Thanks."

Once she was gone, he fixed up his coffee with the cream and sugar it required and then took another look at the photo, a familiar sense of loss and sadness at the failed relationship appearing. Hurt was present as well. It was one thing to be dumped, but to be dumped and replaced so quickly, especially after being together for nearly two years . . . that was really hard. Seeing all the lovey-dovey Facebook statuses between the two only added to the heartbreak.

Jonathan

Jonathan Turner opened his eyes upon a sunlit bedroom and instantly knew something was wrong. Four minutes later, standing in nothing but his pajama pants, he discovered a scattering of bloody feathers where the chickens usually roamed and then, after patrolling the area a bit, found what was left of Charles.

Tears sprang to his eyes as he looked upon the torn body, the realization that he would never again hear the large rooster crowing hitting hard.

Frustration followed.

In response to several coyote sightings Jonathan had spent two entire days beefing up the security of the chicken coup and the fence surrounding the coup area. It had been an expensive task given all the lumber and tools he had needed, yet one he knew was necessary due to the sustenance the hens would provide during the coming winter months.

And it had all been for nothing; the time, energy and money wasted.

It was crazy.

What was worse was that stuff like this kept happening. One thing after another, almost as if all the possible disasters had gotten together and drawn dates on when they wanted to unfold upon him and the farm.

He could picture it perfectly and could hear the statement of *"wouldn't it be funny if . . ."* being repeated over and over again, the only change being the actual event that would be taking place.

But what was the purpose for this?

Growing up he had been taught that things always happened for a reason, and while that reason might never be understood or even revealed, it was still there. He had also been taught that questioning the reasons for things was dangerous.

Just accept that there is a purpose for it, his parents had always said. Even asking what it was God wanted him to learn from the experience was a huge *no no* because if God wanted him to know what it was it would have been made clear to him from the start. *Such questions are a tool of Satan and used to make you a Doubting Thomas.*

Now, however, he couldn't help but ponder the why of things and if that led him down toward an eventual residence in Hell, so be it.

But maybe this is Hell?

Maybe you were in the car with them?

Several seconds of laugher arrived, its echo disappearing off into the withered fields.

Once finished, he realized how ridiculous he was being. This wasn't Hell. It couldn't be. Once there, one wouldn't be questioning whether they were there because it would be obvious.

And be careful.

The purpose of all these disasters could be to see how strong you are.

Some said that God would use an earthly being as his champion against the forces of Satan come the End Times and maybe he was testing him for that position. After all, many agreed that those End Times were drawing near given all the sin and corruption in the world, his parents having been among them.

But thinking it could be you would be a mark against you in

God's eyes, wouldn't it?

Confusion entered his mind.

His parents and grandfather had given him so much information about God and his plan and his ways of working during his lifetime, some of which seemed to come in conflict with earlier pieces of information, that it was hard to keep all the do's and don'ts straight.

Best to not even think about it.

Instead . . .

He focused his attention back upon the situation at hand and realized he was going to have to get more chickens. Of course, he had no idea where to buy them since his family had been breeding them for as long as he could remember, but he was sure someone in town would know. First things first, though, he needed to figure out where the failure in the coup and fence had occurred. No sense rushing out to replace them if they were just going to become a meal once more.

Charles wasn't eaten.

This realization startled him because it once again brought up the question of purpose, only this time he could easily contemplate it without fearing for his soul. The purpose of a coyote working its way into this coup area was to eat. Predators didn't just kill to kill. Yet that was exactly what had occurred. Something had ripped Charles apart, but failed to consume him. *Why?* Was it to silence him so that he wouldn't crow during the attack and wake him?

Can a coyote even think like that?

No, and even if they could, why rip him apart after the fact?

Such actions seemed unnecessary and unlikely, especially for a coyote. He also couldn't picture any other local predator behaving in such a way. In fact, the only thing he could think of when contemplating someone carrying this out was a person, but why would someone come way out here to kill his chickens?

From time to time, his parents had clashed with townspeople, especially in October whenever the town had held Halloween celebrations, but nothing like this had ever resulted from it.

The gate! He twisted around and looked at it. *Had it been standing open?*

Thinking back a few minutes he was sure it had been, but couldn't be one hundred percent certain of it. However, if it had been standing open then that proved a person had been responsible, for no animal could work the latch.

Unless it was a monkey?

But there weren't monkeys in these parts and even if there were, they wouldn't eat chickens.

Looking around he couldn't find any other access point, which made it seem more and more likely that the gate had been used.

But by whom?

Could it have been someone from town?

Or maybe a drifter?

Given the economy which was being slowly destroyed by the Godless heathen in the White House, one who was methodically paving the way for Satan's army, it wouldn't be unlikely that an out of work drifter had come through and eaten his chickens, one who knew enough to kill Charles first so no one would be alerted to the theft.

But why rip Charles apart?

Nothing seemed to explain this, mostly because it seemed very personal and thus something that would have only been carried out by someone who was taking out anger toward him and the farm.

No one stood out as being capable of such actions,

especially considering the lack of conflict with the townspeople now that his parents were gone, and the fact that a hungry drifter wouldn't let anything go to waste.

So . . .

A memory from his youth started to unfold, one that forced him to spin around and then hurry through the gate to look out upon the south field.

Nothing out of the ordinary was present, everything, including the new scarecrow being where it should be. That didn't necessarily mean it hadn't done something during the dark nighttime hours though.

But why would it go back to its post?

Once, when he was young, a scarecrow had come down from its post and tried to kill his family. To this day, he still had nightmares about the event, ones that didn't end with the shotgun blast that had put a stop to the terror that night.

Would it have gone back to its post once it finished us all off?

No answer arrived.

He then tried to push the thought away before the memories of his sister appeared, but couldn't, and, as always, felt tears brewing.

* * *

Fifteen minutes later, once he had gotten control of his emotions, he put on shoes and ventured out into the ruined field to check upon the scarecrow, a shotgun in one hand, a sickle in the other.

Fear at what he might find once he got close was present, but he didn't let it get the better of him.

And then he was there, standing beneath the scarecrow, its round burlap head looking down upon him from about twelve feet above.

Nothing moved.

It appeared lifeless.

But was it?

He prodded it with edge of the sickle, first in the leg and then in the groin.

Nothing.

He then checked the ropes holding it to the post.

They were all tight.

Questions on whether it could tie itself back to the post like this arrived but once again, no answers followed. He simply didn't know enough about scarecrows to arrive at any useful conclusions.

Well, that wasn't completely true. He did know that they could be dangerous during the first week or so after being posted, which was why he had made sure the bindings were secure, but that was it. All the other important pieces of information about these creations had been inside the head of his grandfather who, unfortunately, had died several years earlier after being bitten by a snake in the east field.

It was after that when things had started to go downhill, memories of his father always being drunk and unable to tend to the crops and other situations that required his skills playing across his mind.

All because of Naomi.

Once again, tears arrived.

He had to stop thinking about her.

He had –

Movement caught his eye.

He looked up at the scarecrow, eyes expecting a sudden, swift attack.

Nothing.

Just your imagination.

The thought did little to calm him, which was understandable given the horror he had witnessed all those years ago.

Will it happen again?

As much as he wanted to say no he had a feeling it would, and this time no one else would be around to help defend against it.

And this one was strong.

He had learned that the hard way prior to securing it upon the post, the wound on his arm still bearing witness to the moment when it had fought back.

So be prepared.

The trouble was, the attack would probably arrive while he was sleeping, which would make defending himself difficult.

Unless . . .

He hurried to the barn, the memories of what his father had done to make sure Naomi wouldn't be able to sneak out again having provided him with a possible solution.

Five minutes later, he was heading back into the house to put on some clothes and find some money, his journey into the barn having reminded him that he needed more chain before he could put his solution to work since the last strand of it was still being put to use in the loft.

Saturday, September 1, 2012

Holly

SORRY. RUNNING JUST A TAD BIT LATE. BE
THERE SOON.

Holly read the text and sighed. Being late seemed to be
the norm with Ethan. It didn't matter what the plans were
or how important a specific arrival time was, with him at
the wheel (or really just involved at all) they would be
late. Movies were the worst. They had gone to two since
starting to date in mid June and both times had arrived
after the previews had begun. Thankfully, the theater
hadn't been crowded either time, so finding a seat hadn't
been an issue. Such luck wouldn't always be on her side,
however. At some point something would be released
that would pull in the crowds, something that they would
probably want to go see, and unless she put her foot down
on this lateness issue . . .

Memories of watching people crawling over others in
an attempt to get lone seats between groups during the
opening weekend of *The Hunger Games* played across her
mind's eye.

"See, good thing we got here early," Scott had whispered
during one of these moments.

She hadn't replied, the argument the two had shared

earlier in the evening, one that had actually been sparked by his insistence that they leave an hour before the movie was set to begin, still heavy upon her mind.

You can't win.

What was crazy was that she didn't really mind arriving early for movies, especially ones that promised to be packed, but had been so annoyed with Scott by that point in their crumbling relationship that anything he did irritated her. Plus, he hadn't asked if that time was good. Instead, he just told her that was when he would be picking her up.

Anger sparked.

Let it go.

Doing so was easier said than done, though she wasn't sure why. Never before had the memories from a past relationship, both good and bad, lingered with her for so long. She didn't like it. Even worse, all her girlfriends seemed to think it was because the two were meant to be together. *You were both so cute and perfect for each other,* they had always said, which made talking to them about it impossible. *And all those little things he would do to tell you how much he loved you . . . I wish my guy would do that.*

Her phone beeped.

JUST HAVE TO STOP FOR GAS AND THEN I WILL BE ON MY WAY. SEE YOU SOON.

Jesus Christ! her mind snapped.

See, Scott would have made sure the tank was full the night before, a girlfriend's voice added.

Holly shook her head.

The worst part of all was she knew that if she called Scott and asked him to take her out to help with her project he would say yes without any hesitation. It reminded her of something Amber had told her a few weeks ago about how he had actually turned down two girls who wanted to date him, *girls who would have easily gone to bed with him too.*

Maybe he simply isn't ready yet, Holly had suggested.

No, Amber had said. *He's keeping himself pure and waiting for you two to get back together. It's so sweet.*

It was driving her nuts. Why couldn't they all hate him like girlfriends were supposed to do after a breakup?

She let out another sigh and started checking her camera gear even though she knew it was all ready to go, and then signed onto Facebook to type up a status about heading out to look for scarecrows today.

Five replies using the words WHAT and WHY were posted by the time Ethan's text about being out front arrived, at which point she quickly closed her laptop and headed downstairs, her camera bag slung over one shoulder, her purse over the other.

* * *

"Oh, come on," Holly said as Ethan snapped the picture. "I don't want people seeing me like this."

"You look fine," Ethan said while examining the picture. He turned the phone screen toward her. "See?"

"Oh, gag," Holly said.

"What?" He looked at the screen again and then started working the phone with one hand. "It's great and I bet everyone will agree with me."

"Wait, what're you doing?" she demanded. "You're not posting that are you?"

He smiled.

"Ethan, please don't."

"Too late." He turned the phone toward her again. "Don't worry, everyone will love it."

She didn't reply.

"And just to make sure it has appeared on your wall . . ." he started.

She crossed her arms.

"... there!"

He turned the phone toward her again so she could see the tag he had added. Rather than look at it, she simply glared at him.

Unfazed, he twisted the phone back to himself and said, "Wow, already one like."

"Swell," she said and then turned to look at the waitress who was approaching.

"Ready to order?" she asked.

"Yeah," Ethan said and rattled off an omelet order that seemed to have every ingredient possible within it.

"That all?" Holly asked, waiting.

Ethan gave her an odd look and said, "Um ... white toast, butter on the side."

"And -- " the waitress started, carefully looking between the two " -- that comes with your choice of hash browns or home fries and bacon or sausage."

"Hash browns and bacon."

The waitress wrote all this down and then turned to Holly and said, "For you?"

"Belgian waffle with bacon," Holly said.

"Would you like any fruit on that?"

"Oh ... um ..." she quickly checked to see the price of such an addition since she had agreed to pay for all the expenses on this trip " ... no thanks."

"Okay, I'll be back with some coffee and have that order up in a jiffy." With that, she left the table.

"Two more likes," Ethan said. "Oh, and what a surprise, Scott's picture is one of the eight in your friend box again."

"Big deal."

"You do know that means he is visiting your profile all the time, right? Doesn't that creep you out?"

"Not really, if that's what it actually means." Ethan had mentioned this before in an attempt to get her to unfriend Scott, but after researching it herself she couldn't find any verification of his claim, just speculation from others commenting on it on various forum threads. "Now, if he were posting and commenting on things all the time, then maybe I'd think about removing him, but if he is just looking, that's cool with me."

"That is what it means, though Facebook will never come out and say it." He sipped some coffee. "It really doesn't bother you at all?"

"Nope."

"And if it bothers me?" he asked.

"I'd say . . . tough."

"Really?"

"Seriously, does it bother you?" she asked, voice full of concern.

"Yeah."

"Tough."

His face failed to mirror the grin her own face held, which, for some reason, pleased her even more.

"You really don't care that it bothers me?" he asked, arms crossed.

"Did you care that I asked you not to post the picture?" she countered.

"That's different."

"How?"

"It -- " he stopped as the waitress returned with the coffee pot.

"Look," she said before he could continue. "I'm not one of those girls who will put up with a lot of dating drama. I won't pitch a fit if you're friends with former girlfriends on your profile or if you make comments on their walls and I expect the same courtesy. Scott and I are friends and if you can't deal with that – " she shrugged " – well, its up to you to decide how big of a deal you want to make it."

"I see."

Nothing else was said until their food arrived and then that was just to let the waitress know everything looked good.

* * *

"Scarecrows?" the guy at the hardware store asked. "What in the world you want to take pictures of them for?"

"It's for a college class," Holly said.

"This is what they're teaching you? To go take pictures of scarecrows?"

Holly was caught off guard. "Well . . . this is just a photo class I decided to take. The others have more serious subjects."

He gave her a suspicious look and then said, "Well, if scarecrows are what you're looking for I can tell you to head up north of town. A couple farms up that way might have some up still, though you'd be better off coming back in the spring once the seeds are planted. That's when they're needed the most, not that they really do much. Putting some sticks in the ground with plastic bags attached works much better at scaring birds away. Even a single strand of ribbon that can be caught in the wind will spook them. A scarecrow just gives them another place to sit and wait."

Holly didn't like the direction this was taking and was starting to wonder if she had chosen the right subject for her project. At the time, it had seemed like such a great idea, especially since NIU was out in the middle of farm country. "But there are some up there, some that I can take pictures of?" she asked.

"Yeah, I've seen a couple from the road," he confirmed. "I don't think you're gonna be all that impressed though. These aren't like the one you see in *Wizard of Oz* or other movies. Nothing more than stick figures slapped together with some old ratty clothes."

Wonderful, her mind said. "Well, thank you."

"No problem. Hope you find one that works for your picture. You know, if you really want to see some nice ones you should probably go into the suburbs where they have those fake farms and pumpkin patches. Those places put a lot of time into things like that since it's all just for show."

"I'll keep that in mind," Holly said. "Thanks."

He nodded.

She left the store and headed back to the car where Ethan was waiting.

"So?" he asked.

"They basically told me we should head to Sunny Acers out in West Chicago because people in these parts are more likely to put a stick with a bag on it than build a scarecrow."

"Oh."

Silence settled.

"What do you want to do?" he asked after nearly a minute.

"Well, he did say there might be some to the north of town. Nothing spectacular, but at least it will be something so I can show some progress come Tuesday."

"So, head up that way then?" he asked.

"Yeah."

"And hey, if we don't find something good at least we had a wonderful breakfast at a cool little diner, right," he said, voice cheery.

"Yeah."

"And tomorrow we can head to Sunny Acers."

Ethan

"That *was* the driveway!" Holly said.

"Are you sure?" Ethan asked. "It wasn't even paved."

"Yeah, well, not everyone paves things out here. Didn't you see the mailbox?"

"No."

"How could you miss it," she demanded. "It was huge."

"I was paying attention to the road."

Holly didn't reply to that and instead said, "Well, find a spot to turn around."

"Okay . . . or I could just pull over up here and you can run into the field and snap the picture."

He felt the glare before he saw it and turned toward her.

"What?" he asked.

"Just snap the picture," she said, anger evident. "Is that how you view my photo work?"

"I . . . well . . ." *crap!*

"Well?"

"Of course not," he said while slowing the car for a stop sign, voice trying to keep cool. "I know there's more to it than that. I just didn't realize . . ." *didn't realize what?* Nothing came to mind.

Holly waited.

Ethan made a right turn at the four way stop, but rather than continuing down that road, he quickly pulled the car to the left for a large U-turn in the middle of the intersection. The maneuver was dangerous and illegal, but given that there was no traffic, he felt the risk was okay.

"Didn't realize what?" Holly pressed.

Ethan sighed. "I misspoke, okay. I'm sorry. Can we just move on?"

Holly didn't reply and simply crossed her arms and turned to look out the window, her continued glare momentarily reflecting back at him from the glass.

So glad I agreed to this trip, Ethan said to himself. Nothing was better than waking up early on a Saturday to drive a bitchy girl all over the place. *And just think, you could have been hanging out with Jed and Brandon behind the house.* Chances were one or both would have some nice grass to smoke too thanks to a connection with someone near the Fox River over in Geneva who was growing it in their basement apartment (who knew the soil there could produce such a fine taste?). Of course, smoking that with them would mean he had to break his vow with Holly who forbid such activities, but that was okay since it seemed unlikely that she would indulge him in the 'cornfield shenanigans' they had talked about the other night.

"If I get a good jump on all my pictures and we're both still feeling up to it, then maybe we could try that," she had teased.

Probably never intended to go through with it anyway, he now concluded. *Better start putting out more or else I'm going too –*

"Stop, stop, stop," Holly urged as a guy with a big,

unrestrained dog stepped out into the driveway.

Ethan pressed the brakes and listened as the gravel beneath the car fought the tires.

"Can you go tell him why we're here?" Holly asked once the car was stopped.

"What? I'm not going out there with that dog."

"Are you serious?"

"Are you?"

Holly shook her head and opened the door.

Though obviously interested, the dog never left the man's side.

Fuck, you should have just gone out there, Ethan said as Holly walked up and explained what they were doing. He watched the man chuckle and then nod.

Holly then turned and gave him an encouraging wave and said, "It's okay, the dog won't bite you." To prove this, or maybe to add to his humiliation, she reached down and petted the dog's head, the words, "Such a good little boy," echoing in a squeaking baby voice.

Ethan sighed and opened the door to step out. While doing this he heard the man say, "So, you all want to take pictures of the scarecrows. Never had anyone want to do that before. Makes me wish I had done a better job when building them."

With that the man led them out into the field, his voice cautioning them about the footing several times both due to all the foot snagging trip points and the possibility of snakes.

"Really?" Ethan asked about the latter, a chill racing though him.

"Yep," the man said. "Seen two this month already. Lots of rodents out and about looking for food cause of the drought which brings out the snakes who want to fatten up before winter."

"Great," Ethan muttered. This trip was just getting better and better.

* * *

"Like I said, it's not much, but it does the trick," the man said.

Not much is right, Ethan said to himself. With the right items, he could have built something just like it in ten minutes and propped it up in one of the fields off Peace Road for Holly to take a picture of.

"It's perfect," Holly said.

"Really?"

"Yeah, see, everyone always thinks these things are really elaborate, but that's because the only ones most ever see are in movies or at tourist traps. My photos will show people what they are really like."

Thrown together pieces of crap, Ethan silently voiced.

"Well, I suppose that is important," the man said, hands going into his pockets. He watched for a moment as Holly opened her camera bag. "So, um, you need me for anything or can I go back?"

"Oh, no," Holly said. "We should be fine."

"Okay. Well. I'll be in the barn back there if you need anything."

"Thanks. Oh, do you mind if we go to the other scarecrow out in that field too once we're done here?" She pointed off into the distance where one stood.

"Not at all, though it's pretty much the same as this one." He shrugged.

Holly nodded. "Well, I'll see how much film we use on this one."

Being forced to use film rather than digital for the class was a huge plus in Ethan's eyes because it gave a stopping point for the pictures. On the downside it meant Holly was going to be very careful with each shot, her eyes making sure each one was set up perfectly before snapping the picture and moving on to another angle, all while he watched with nothing to do.

Bring a book, she had suggested.

Yeah, because reading is my favorite pastime, he had sarcastically replied. The funny thing was he had brought a book just in case things did get boring, one written by the writer guy over in Sycamore who had been in the news last year due to a very bizarre stalking and murder thing that had occurred with a female NIU student that lived below him.

"Oh, by the way," the guy said before heading back to the barn. "Believe it or not, voices don't carry out here very well, so if something should happen like a snake bite or anything, don't bother trying to yell, just run to me as fast as you can, okay?"

"Oh . . . kay," Holly said.

Ethan nodded. "Thanks."

"No problem." He turned and started walking away.

"That was creepy," Ethan admitted once the man was out of earshot.

"Yeah," Holly agreed. "I don't know about you, but I keep looking for snakes now every time I move."

"Me too."

"And we probably won't see a single one."

"Hope not." It reminded him of when his family went snorkeling in Hawaii. His fear of sharks had made him see a fin with every wave that drifted by.

He watched as she carefully loaded a roll of film into the camera and then started checking things with it.

"Need me to do anything?"

"Um . . . nope." She looked through the viewfinder for a moment and then added, "Unless you want to hold the bag so that no snakes crawl in and surprise us in the car later."

He chuckled a bit even though the thought gave him another chill.

* * *

"I have to admit, I hope we do find some that are a little bit more impressive than this one was," Holly said forty minutes later once the camera was back in the bag.

"I know what you mean," Ethan said, and then almost voiced his earlier thought about slapping one together himself for her, but then thought better of it.

"I mean, it's great that it's authentic and everything, but still . . ." she lifted her arms and glanced over at the scarecrow, which consisted of a work shirt buttoned over a cross made out of two thin pieces of wood with a hat on top.

He nodded and then asked, "You want to go to the next one over there or try to find a better one on another farm?"

"Better one."

"Okay."

With that, the two headed back to the car, a quick detour to thank the man who was in the barn fixing something taking place.

"You get all the pictures you need?" he asked while wiping his hand on a rag.

"Yep, for this one," Holly said. "Still need to find several more though for the project. Any suggestions on local farms that might have some?"

"Oh, that's a tough one. Some of people around here will have something up for the winter wheat. Not sure if you'll find anything more elaborate than the ones I have, but . . ."

Holly waited.

". . . well, you never know what you might find out there. Wish I could be more helpful."

"Hey, just letting me take pictures of the ones you have was great and very helpful, so no worries."

He smiled.

"Yep, thank you so much. Hopefully everyone will be as willing to allow us the opportunity to take pictures as you have been," Ethan said. He then turned to Holly and added, "We should probably get moving if we want to capture some more shots."

"He's right," the man said. "Getting darker earlier and earlier these days, so you'll want to get as much in as possible before that sun sets. Good luck."

"All right, well, thanks again," Holly said and then turned with Ethan to head back to the car.

A few minutes later they were at the end of the driveway, Ethan asked, "Which way."

"I have no idea. How about go right and then take a left at that stop sign."

"Sounds good."

Saturday, September 15, 2012

Scott

"My niece says you were looking for those two kids that wanted to see scarecrows," the older lady behind the register said.

Scott nodded. "Yeah, that's right."

"Might I ask why?"

He pulled out his credit card and handed it over and then said, "They never came home that day so I'm trying to figure out what happened."

She looked at him for a moment and then ran the credit card through the machine.

"The police won't get involved," he added, anticipating her next question.

"Oh? And why not?" She had a skeptical tone to her voice, which suddenly made him wonder if maybe she had given Holly and Ethan a location for finding scarecrows, but was unsure if she should reveal it to him.

"Because no bodies have turned up and their car has not been found. Nothing for them to go on and since they are both adults . . ." he shrugged ". . . nothing they can really do but issue a missing persons report."

She pondered this for a moment while the old credit card machine processed everything, and then, once it was ready, handed him a receipt to sign along with his credit card.

Scott wrote in a five-dollar tip, totaled up everything, and signed his name.

She took the merchant copy and said, "I did offer them a suggestion while they were here."

"Really?"

She nodded. "I told them they might have better luck over at the hardware store. The guy that owns that, his name is Ray; he knows all the local farm families pretty well and would have had a better idea on where one could find scarecrows."

"Wow, okay, and where is that exactly?"

"Just down the road a ways. You can't miss it."

"Excellent. Thank you so much." He noticed Sophia standing close, listening in and offered her a smile.

"I hope you find them," Sophia said.

"Thanks, me too."

"Might I make a suggestion," the aunt said. "We have a deputy from over in Wilton stationed here during the day who might be able to help you. And even if he can't give you any information, he might be able to help in contacting local farmers who may have come in contact with your friends."

"Oh, that might not be a bad idea," Scott said, humoring her. "Where is the police department located?"

"Well, the town doesn't actually have a police force anymore -- can't afford it -- but the Wilton department has a deputy here during the day over in an office behind the old bookstore."

"Oh wow, how does the town respond to emergencies when the deputy isn't working?" Scott asked. He had never heard of anything like this before, but wondered if it was common in small towns given how broke the state was.

"Wilton deputies do routine patrols through the area at night, and some during the day, and any 911 calls are routed through their dispatch."

"I see," he said with a nod. "Thanks again. I will certainly contact them if I need help talking to people. By chance, do you know of any farm that has a scarecrow that is so well done that my friends would have been told by everyone they had to go see it?"

The aunt shook her head. "Sorry."

* * *

"Yeah, I remember her," the man who Scott guessed was named Ray said while looking at the picture. "Came in asking about scarecrows, right?"

"Yes, exactly," Scott said, hope rising. His theory that the scarecrow topic would be remembered by everyone who was asked given its uniqueness was panning out. "Were you able to tell them about any specific locations they might have gone to see them at?"

He shook his head. "Now that I couldn't do. The idea that every farm has some elaborate scarecrow watching over things isn't really accurate, so all I could do was suggest she head north to check out some of the farms up there."

"Okay. So there are farms up there then that would have some scarecrows?"

"Yeah, but like I said, nothing she would really want to take pictures of. These are all working farms so everything they use is very practical. Why build something elaborate when a simple shirt stretched over a small cross would be just as effective?"

"Well, believe it or not she probably would have still wanted to check them out and take pictures," Scott said. A sad smile followed, one that was brought about by memories of some of the mini adventures the two had gone on during their time together.

"If you think so then all I can suggest is you head north and talk to some of the farmers up there and see if they remember her."

Scott nodded.

"By the way, it's none of my business really, but why are you looking for them?"

Scott had been wondering if this question would pop up. In fact, he anticipated it from everyone he talked too simply because it seemed almost second nature to ask WHY when it appeared one person was looking for another -- especially if that other person was a pretty young lady. As expected, a suggestion on talking to the local deputy followed his explanation.

"Where exactly is Wilton?" Scott asked after agreeing to take the advice and speak with the deputy.

"Um, bout eight miles south of here if you're talking the downtown area."

"And the deputies from there come all the way up here to patrol at night?"

"Well, it's not like they park themselves up here, but the ones on duty during the night make a couple regular patrols through the area. And then we always have one in town during the day."

"Do you think it would be possible for my friends to have gotten their car stuck somewhere and for it to have gone undiscovered for two weeks?"

He considered this for several seconds, nodded, and said, "If they got themselves stuck in a really rural area that no one travels, or that no one could see them from if they did travel the nearby road, then yeah, it's possible. But at the same time all they'd have to do is walk a few miles in any direction and they would come upon a well traveled road or a farm or even back here to town." He shrugged and added a simple, "So . . ."

"That's supposing they could walk after an incident," Scott said.

No reply, unless one counted the solemn look the man gave.

* * *

A few minutes later, while sitting in his car in the hardware store parking lot, Scott was overwhelmed by a sense of hopelessness. Finding the town had been one thing; but now locating Holly was another.

What did you expect?

No answer arrived, mostly because he hadn't really thought much beyond his goal of locating the town, and when he did, he just saw himself asking around until he uncovered something.

And if it were that simple –

He shook the thought away.

Going around and asking people about them was all one could do. Hell, it's what the police would do if they had decided this case was something that needed their attention. After all, people didn't just vanish into thin air. Someone somewhere was the last person to see them, and whatever information they could give him might spark an idea of where they were.

An image of them sitting in a smashed up car in a ditch somewhere that was shielded from the road entered his mind, and, despite how horrible such a discovery would be, he knew it would at least be an answer. In fact, given the time that had passed, chances were the answer wasn't going to be pleasant.

Jonathan

He felt hundreds of eyes on him as he drove into town, memories of all the past conflicts between his family and the townspeople playing across his mind. Of course, he couldn't see any of those people watching him, but knew they were there, his mother's statements about how people like them were always being observed echoing loud and clear.

Sinners will always be watching us in hope that they can catch us doing something sinful, she had often said. *Never mind that they don't follow God's law themselves, and will never be as close to him as we are, they just like to point out our shortcomings and failures.*

Sometimes Satan was watching as well through those sinner's eyes hoping to not only see them in a moment of weakness, but capitalize upon it in order to capture their souls.

Just like Naomi.

He sighed.

No matter how much he tried, thoughts of her kept intruding upon him, all thanks to the scarecrow and the possibility that it was planning an attack. Had it not been for that he could have easily gone about his day without thinking about her or the near ruin she had brought upon the family; all because she had been seduced by the evil within the town, one that had been much too strong for the family to purge from her.

What was really upsetting about the whole thing was that she had been warned time and time again about how she was more susceptible to Satan and his evil influence given her womanhood, yet had still secretly gone into town several times without a male escort. It was sad. Unfortunately, there was nothing he, or the family, had been able to do about it. *There'll always be those that question too much and defy God,* his mother had said after all was said and done. *Even some who share our blood. We did the best we could with her.*

Jonathan nodded as if the statement were being spoken, and then guided the car into the parking lot of the hardware store.

'We did the best we could,' his mind repeated, an image of the bell his father had chained around Naomi's neck appearing before his mind's eye.

Always the clever one, Naomi had simply taped the bell down so it would not jingle, thus allowing her to keep leaving the house at night. Thankfully, the scarecrow wouldn't be able to do such a thing, at least not without going inside and finding some tape. By then he would hear the bell ringing and would have the shotgun ready.

Unless there is some tape in the barn somewhere?

He would have to do a thorough search once he got back. In the meantime, he needed a good length of chain.

And ask where you can buy some new chickens.

* * *

"Wouldn't surprise me," Ray said. "Those coyotes can be tricky little bastards."

Jonathan winced at the profanity, but also nodded in agreement. Had it been anyone else using such a word he wouldn't have cared, but Ray was someone he actually felt a connection to given how kind and helpful he always was, so he hated the thought of him having to burn in hell for eternity. Not that he would say anything. His family had learned long ago that it just wasn't worth it to try to change the ways of the world. *Best we prepare our family and make sure we are ready for the trials and tribulations that are about to be unleashed.*

The End Times were coming and unlike many who identified with the Christian religion, his family didn't believe in the idea of the rapture.

Nope, that is a falsehood created by a few who were misled, his parents had often said. *We are a part of God's army and will be expected to fight in the coming battles. It will be the ultimate test of our faith, one that will bring ruin down among many who claim to be Christians.*

"So, I'm going to need to pick up some more chickens too, but am not really sure where to get them. Does anyone around here sell them?"

"In town? Not right now. You'll have to go talk to some of your neighbors and see if they're willing to part with any full grown ones."

"I see."

"Or maybe go buy a carton of eggs from the grocery store and put them under a heat lamp."

"Does that really work?" Jonathan asked.

Ray stared at him for several second and then shook his head. "No, not at all. It was a joke."

"Ah." Jonathan chuckled to mask the embarrassment he felt. Eggs were not something his family ever bought from the grocery store, and the ones that were laid on the farm would produce chickens if they weren't picked up.

"By the way, you didn't happen to have any visitors a while back? A guy and a girl looking for scarecrows."

The question caused his bowels to quiver. "W-what?"

"I know, it sounds pretty silly, but there was a girl who

was looking to take pictures of scarecrows for a class and it seems she went missing while doing it."

Jonathan didn't know what to say. Being questioned about the girl was the last thing he had expected when coming to town.

"Anyhow, some guy is now looking for her and will probably pay you a visit at some point today."

"Why me?" he gasped.

Ray gave him a puzzled look, one that faded after a few seconds and said, "He's going around to several of the farms hoping to find out where she went."

"Is he with the police?" His voice was better this time, calmer.

"No, in fact, I think it might be like a brother or a boyfriend or something." He shrugged. "You know, someone who is taking matters into their own hands."

Once again, Jonathan wasn't sure how to reply. In fact, the only thing he could think about now was getting back to the house because the last thing he wanted was for the guy to arrive there and start nosing around.

Ray looked as if he might say more, but then the bell above the door jingled as someone came in.

Hearing this helped Jonathan steer the conversation back toward his purchase, the words, "How much?" leaving his lips.

"Just the chain?" Ray asked.

"Yeah."

He checked the length, punched some figures into the register, and said, "Five thirty seven."

Jonathan nodded and handed him six crumbled up singles and then did a quick glance down the aisle behind him to see who had entered the store, but whoever it was, they had disappeared down a different aisle.

"Oh, by the way, if you keep having trouble with the

coyotes come on back and I'll show you some new stuff that might help," Ray said while handing him his change.

"Okay." Jonathan said, uninterested. Though he had agreed with Ray that it probably had been coyotes, inside he knew this wasn't the case. Telling him it had been the scarecrow, however, would have raised too many questions and might have even brought people out to the farm. Always best to keep that information to himself.

And we won't tell anyone about what happened tonight, right? his grandfather had said all those years ago, the dead scarecrow lying in the hallway.

I won't tell.

Good boy. And just in case you forget, do you know what will happen if you do tell? People will come and take you away from your mommy and daddy, and you don't want that, do you.

Nope. That had been one of his biggest fears while growing up. Being taken away and forced to live in a sinful house that would ultimately lead him to an eternity in Hell. Even the worst moments of punishment his family inflicted upon him for certain deeds were nothing compared to such a fate.

And remember, we're doing this so you don't go to Hell, his mother had once said, his knees already screaming in agony just from the few minutes of kneeling on the hard rice grains in the kitchen corner. *You understand that, right?*

Yes, he had said, tears running down his face.

As it turned out that had been a mild punishment compared to other things his parents had done during the course of his childhood, yet at the time those three hours on the rice had seemed like the worst possible thing one could ever endure.

Root cellar.

Snakes.

He pushed the memory away as he got into the car, his mind not wanting to think about that horrible week back when he was eleven.

* * *

Twenty minutes later he was home, chain, cowbell, and ladder all balanced in one hand, shotgun in the other, feet taking him to the scarecrow once again.

While driving he had feared that he would come upon the young man that Ray had talked about, but no one was there when he had pulled up and nothing had been disturbed.

But that doesn't mean he won't show up and if he does . . .

At the moment he wasn't sure what he would do, but did know there were some precautions he needed to take just in case. First things first, however, he would focus on the scarecrow.

Maybe just shoot it now?

Would that work?

Once again, he wished he knew more about these things, but, alas, he didn't.

The bell will work.

Memories of watching his father padlock the chain around Naomi's neck as she screamed at them entered his mind once more. Hearing it at the time had caused him to cry. Later his parents had explained to him why such a step had been necessary.

Looking back, he knew that her continued defiance had been the reason why his punishments had always been so severe. After what happened to her, his parents weren't going to take any chances with him. Even going to school like Naomi had done was out. Too risky.

An odd mix of hatred and appreciation arrived while thinking about this, along with an inner statement telling him it had all been for the best.

And now . . .

He approached the scarecrow carefully, eyes looking for signs of life.

Nothing.

Still, he would not let his guard down and kept the shotgun ready as he prepared everything. He then went up the ladder, which was set behind the scarecrow so that it wouldn't see him setting down the shotgun for a moment when he wrapped the chain around its neck.

Done!

He nearly jumped down from the ladder in an effort to get away once the padlock was secure, but managed to control himself enough to carefully step down each rung, his mind knowing he didn't want to jump onto an uneven surface with dry corn crops all around. Too easy to break an ankle or a leg and then the bell would only serve to let him know that the scarecrow was coming for him as he tried to crawl away.

Saturday, September 1, 2012

Holly

Her pictures were horrible. At least, this was her assumption based on the small screen images she quickly scrolled through while Scott backed out of the third driveway they had shot at. And it wasn't the lack of artistic design that went into the scarecrows that proved the downfall of the pictures. Instead, it was her photo skills, or lack there of. Others who knew what they were doing could probably have created masterpieces with this subject matter, ones that spoke volumes on the simplicity of farm life and the necessity of keeping things practical. Her photos, however, spoke volumes on how difficult it was to take good pictures and how advanced technology didn't nullify the need for talent and skill.

"Oh, come on, they can't be that bad," Ethan said when she voiced her disgust a few seconds later. By then they were making their way to the crossroads that helped create the border between two farms, one being the farm they had just finished with.

"They are," she grumbled.

"Well, even if they are, you can always make them look great with a computer."

She shook her head.

"What?" he asked.

"Nothing."

She felt his stare for several seconds, and for a moment

almost snapped at him about how he never listened and should have known that the whole point of this was to take shots that would be developed upon traditional film despite the digital technology of the camera, but then kept it all to herself.

You always kept things to yourself with Scott when you should have spoken up, her mind warned.

Yeah, another part countered. *But I loved him.*

The reply startled her a bit because it was the first time she had ever admitted this to herself. With it came the realization that she and Ethan had no real future.

"Okay, see anything?" Ethan asked as he turned down the road that took them alongside a new farm.

Holly stared out her window at the field, her eyes only able to see a small portion due to the severe slope that ran down the middle.

"Nothing," she said after a minute. "But there might be something out there beyond that slope on the other side."

"Want me to turn around and see if we can find a road that takes us around it?" he offered.

"Um . . . no, just keep going." A new farm would probably appear soon beyond the next intersection, wherever that was.

"Okay."

Five minutes later, they came upon a river that forced a northward bend in the road. Beyond the river was nothing but a tangled mess of trees.

"Looks like we'll still get to see the other side of that farm after all," Ethan said.

"If the road turns that way," Holly muttered.

* * *

As it happened there was no road that would take them along the northern edge of the farm they had been driving alongside, nor did there appear to be a farm beyond it, just unwanted scrubland.

"So, now what?" Ethan asked. He had pulled the car onto what could be considered a shoulder, though it didn't give enough space for them to clear the road. "Want me to turn around?"

"Is there a second option?" Holly asked. She knew she was being irritable, but couldn't help it. Today was not going the way she had wanted it too. Adding to her frustration, she kept thinking about Scott and how the two probably would have had a good time during this trip even with the lack of detailed scarecrows and photo taking abilities. At least they would have before all the drama had started. That had been one of the great things about dating him, she always seemed to have a good time when with him no matter the situation. Hell, even standing in line at the DMV together would have been enjoyable.

"Um, three options actually," Ethan said. "Go forward, or we could get out here and walk into the field a bit and see if we can spot anything once we're atop that rise."

"This isn't exactly a parking spot."

"I'm sure I can find an area that will work."

"Fine."

Ethan didn't act right away, the car staying right where it was.

"Well?" she asked as the clock turned over into a new hour.

"Now that I'm thinking about it, there is a forth option."

"Which is?"

"We call it quits and head home."

She actually considered it, but then said, "No, I need more shots, even if they all suck."

"Okay, well, just so you know, I may simply decide we're done if you keep being a bitch."

Bitch! She couldn't believe her ears. Never once had Scott, or any other boyfriend before this, used such a word to describe her, not even during any of their bitter all night long arguments.

"Just keep that in mind," he added and started to pull the car back into the road.

Holly opened the door.

"Hey!" he cried while hitting the brakes. "What are – "

Holly stepped out and started down into the little drainage ditch.

"Holly, wait," she heard as she hopped over the cracked earth at the bottom and started up the small pre-field slope. "HOLLY!"

She stopped and turned. The car was partway off the road and dangerously close to sliding down into the dried up drainage ditch.

"What?" she demanded.

She expected him to apologize, because that seemed pretty standard in a situation like this, but instead he said, "Don't throw a fit and storm off like a spoiled brat."

Oh, we are so through, she said to herself while turning and continuing up the small rise, feet struggling against the dead clumps of grass.

A question on whether or not Ethan followed entered her mind, but she didn't look back to find out and soon had stepped over the top of the small rise and was in the field, eyes noting that whatever had once grown in this section had long since withered.

Fortunately, this meant she could see quite a distance, and would be able to see even more once she made it to the top of the rise in the field, which looked to be about a three-minute walk from her where she stood.

* * *

"What?" Ethan asked, voice somewhat startled.

"We need to head back and find the driveway to this farm!" she repeated, excitement having momentarily replaced her anger.

"Wait, what'd you see?"

She took several deep breaths, the run back to the car more than she was used too and having taken quite a bit out of her.

Ethan started the car while waiting for the explanation, but didn't pull out right away.

"I couldn't tell for sure, but it looks like this place could actually have the potential for a really decent scarecrow."

"What do you mean by decent?"

"Arms, legs, a round head." She took another couple breaths. "Something that actually looks like a scarecrow."

"You saw this?"

"Well . . . no, but they had a huge empty post with a crossbeam sitting in the middle of the field."

"But no actual scarecrow on it?"

"No, but with such a setup I'm thinking they probably usually have something pretty spectacular, and maybe they moved it to another field or something, maybe for that winter wheat that one guy was talking about." She had no idea what winter wheat was, but figured it required planting and if scarecrows were used to keep birds from eating seeds, then it seemed logical that one might be in use now – if this was the time that winter wheat was planted. She didn't know. Having seen that post, however, she knew the potential was there for a great scarecrow and didn't want to miss it if her theory proved true.

"Maybe . . ." Ethan said, doubt present.

"If nothing else, I could get pictures of the post since it would be scarecrow themed," she added, though deep down inside she hoped this wasn't all she left with while visiting that farm.

"I suppose."

"Let's go."

"Okay, okay." He looked back to make sure no one was using the road and started the process of turning the car around.

* * *

"This must be it," Ethan said.

"Yeah," Holly agreed.

The two were staring at a narrow strip of dirt that just barely bridged the gap over the drainage ditch, both sides showing signs of erosion. Once beyond the ditch the dirt path quickly disappeared around a bend of what looked like some sort of prairie weed that had been allowed to grow freely followed by a thick line of trees.

"Mailbox is a good sign."

"Yeah," she said again. For some reason she was starting to get an uneasy feeling about this place, though she couldn't pinpoint why. Whatever it was however she wasn't about to let it ruin her chances of locating a decent scarecrow. Nope. As far as she was concerned, they had no choice. Whether or not this trip had been worthwhile was going to depend on the shots she was able to capture in the next hour. Of that, she was certain.

Ethan

"Jesus Christ," Ethan said as they crossed the homemade dirt bridge that stretched over the drainage ditch. "Did you feel that?"

"Yeah," Holly said, hand still pressed against the dashboard. "Felt like the right side was about to give way." She twisted around to look back through the rear window. "It didn't actually go, did it?"

Ethan looked back as well, but couldn't tell much from the angle they were positioned at. "I don't know." He opened the door and got out to check. "Looks okay for now, but we better tell whoever lives here that they'll want to reinforce it after we leave because it's not going to take many more crossings, especially if they're driving a truck over it rather than a car like us."

"Oh yeah," Holly agreed. "I didn't even think of that."

"Actually, I'm pretty surprised it's been allowed to get this bad," Ethan added. "Guess the family doesn't leave the place that often."

"Or they have a second driveway."

Ethan hadn't really considered that, but now that the possibility had been suggested he figured it was probably the reason why this one had been allowed to get so bad. Rather than admit that, however, he said, "Or the place is abandoned. Actually, you said the field on the other side had gone to rot, right?"

"Yeah."

"Then there you have it, the place is probably abandoned given the economy."

"Well, I guess that'll make seeing a scarecrow easier."

"If there is one and if it isn't falling apart."

"There will be," she said, the words an attempt to convince herself as well as him given her growing fear that they wouldn't find anything.

"I hope you're right."

She sighed and said, "We'll know soon enough."

"Yeah."

Nothing else was said after that, and, for a moment, Ethan wondered what the point of the little spat had been, but then decided it didn't even matter.

* * *

"Um . . . I'm leaning more and more toward the idea that this place is abandoned," Ethan said once the farmhouse and barn came into view around the bend of trees.

"Then who's taking care of those chickens over there?" Holly asked.

"Oh," he mumbled after following the direction of her gaze. "Didn't see those." Instead, his eyes had been fixated on the hole in the roof; one that he didn't think would have gone unrepaired if the place had been occupied, not when people who owned farms were supposed to be so handy.

"And I'm guessing the cornfield just looks this way due to the drought," she added.

"Could be." Again, chances were good that she was correct, but he didn't want to simply give in and agree. "So, you still want to give this place a try?"

Her lack of a reply was a reply in itself and he took his foot off the brake and continued toward the large area of gravel-laced dirt that sat between the house and barn. While doing this he kept his eyes open for a second driveway, but didn't see anything that connected to the route they were on, nor did he believe there would be a path that would cut through the fields that encircled three sides of the house and barn. Also lacking were any signs of life beyond what was waddling about in the area outside the chicken coup.

But maybe that's because the owners have decided to go get supplies to repair the driveway near the drainage ditch and the hole in the roof?

The silent suggestion had merit, yet didn't ring true for some reason.

"No truck or anything," he said after a few seconds.

"Maybe they keep it in the barn?"

"Maybe," he agreed, right foot bringing the car to a stop between the two structures. "So . . ."

Rather than jump out right away Holly started scanning the area through the windows, her eyes seeming to study every inch of the surrounding landscape.

Ethan waited, his mind noting that she too was apprehensive about this location.

But why?

The question was as much for himself as it was for her since he too had an uneasy feeling.

No answer arrived.

We should just leave.

Giving voice to the thought would have pushed Holly toward stepping out of the car, so he kept it to himself. Sadly, he knew the reverse of this – suggesting they get started – wouldn't have the opposite effect of making her want to leave.

And heaven help him if he simply made that decision for the two of them. It wouldn't matter that deep down inside she actually wanted to leave. After a couple of days she wouldn't even remember her own apprehension and instead would convince herself that she had had every intention of getting the photos taken but was prevented from doing so.

Probably would blame you for her failing grade on the project as well.

He sighed.

"I think I'm going to go knock on the door and see if anyone is home," Holly said.

"Okay," Ethan replied, disappointment entering his system.

"And if no one is home we can leave a note on the car or door or something telling them what we are doing, just in case they pull up while we are out there." She waited a second and then added, "You think that would be a good idea?"

He shrugged. "Probably, though I'm not sure we should really go into their field if they aren't home. That could be . . . well, it just doesn't seem right."

"Yeah," she said.

It took several more seconds for her to open the door and step out.

Once that happened he opened his door and followed.

Nothing was said as they started toward the front door of the house, the only audible sound that arose being the creaks from the rotting steps they used to get up to the door.

The two exchanged glances, a silent question on who would knock passing between them.

Ethan decided to take the lead on this and rapped his knuckles three times against the wood, the second two strikes being the only ones firm enough for someone inside to hear.

They waited.

Nothing.

Holly knocked next and then looked for a bell to press, but didn't see one.

"Well?" Ethan asked.

Holly looked around and then said, "The empty post was that way I believe," and pointed toward the field beyond the left side of the house. "So if they have another post with a scarecrow it would probably be over there somewhere." Her finger pointed to the right beyond the barn.

"Um . . . I really don't know if it is such a good idea to simply head out into the fields," Ethan said, concern rising.

Holly considered this and said, "Maybe you should stay by the car and see if someone comes back while I look around. That way you can explain to them what we're doing and give me a call if they want us to leave."

"I'm more worried about you getting lost out there in the field."

"Are you serious?" she asked. "I'm not going to get lost."

"Holly, these fields are huge and you can't even see if there is a scarecrow out there."

"What about the post I saw?" she asked.

"I'm sure it had a scarecrow on it at one time, and probably will again, but that doesn't mean there is one somewhere else."

She didn't reply.

"Look, I know you're not happy with the photos you've taken, but the project isn't going to be due until what, mid October?"

"Yeah," she muttered.

"So that gives you plenty of time to find more farms

and of course you can always come back to this one at
some point to see if anyone is home and ask them if they
have one for you to see."

She considered this, and, for a moment, he thought she
was going to voice agreement, and that they would be on
their way home, but then, "Let's wait around for a bit and
see if they come home, that way we won't have to drive all
the way out here again just to ask a question."

He sighed. "Okay."

Silence settled.

"Are you able to change your project?" Ethan asked
after a couple of minutes had passed, his mind hoping the
question wouldn't lead to another little spat.

"Why?"

"I was just thinking, we've seen a lot of interesting barn
structures and farm equipment and whatnot, all of which
would probably make interesting photos."

"Yeah, well, only if I had talent at taking them," she
muttered.

"Who cares about talent? You enjoy taking pictures
and the more you do it the better you'll get at it."

"Thanks for the vote of confidence."

"What?"

"You don't get it."

"You're right, I don't," he said after some hesitation. "I
don't get how everything I say, no matter how helpful I'm
trying to be, get's twisted into being negative and
hurtful."

"Telling me I have no talent, you think that's being
helpful?"

"*You* said you had no talent!"

"But *you* agreed!"

He shook his head and turned to look at the house.

Behind him gravel crunched, followed by the sound of

the car door opening.

"What're you doing?" he asked as she retrieved her camera bag.

"Going to take some pictures of this place."

"Don't you need permission?"

"You just suggested I take pictures," she snapped.

He held up his hands and said, "Okay, okay, go take pictures."

"Thank you," Holly said, voice harsh, and started walking around the area, eyes seeming to scan things.

Never again, Ethan said to himself while crossing his arms and leaning against the car. *Next time she needs help she is on her own, or she can call Scott. He'd help her. She could suddenly decide to go get some special hotdog out in the New Jersey and he wouldn't hesitate to drive her there.*

And she knows it.

He could tell. That was why she wouldn't remove him from her friends list on Facebook. She liked the idea of him obsessing over her. She liked –

Movement caught his eye and he turned to see the front door of the house opening.

Saturday, September 15, 2012

Scott

Scanning the fields for scarecrows and the ditches for a car proved to be a difficult task while driving; especially on the narrow roads that twisted left and right so frequently it might as well have been part of a theme park ride. He also seemed to be going too slow for the other drivers who occasionally crept up on him, his attempts at scanning things while keeping his car on the road making it so his speed never really made it over forty miles an hour.

A long horn honk echoed as a dirt-splattered pickup truck darted around him in a no passing zone, the driver managing to cut back over into the right lane seconds before the road made a blind curve to the left. No cars appeared in the oncoming traffic lane as the road beyond the curve was revealed, but if one had, things could have been messy – even without an actual collision between the two. Simply being startled and slamming on the brakes at these speeds could prove disastrous. Scott knew this from experience. His one and only accident had occurred a year earlier when he had crushed the brakes to miss a cat crossing Route 23 and spun out of control into a tree. Thankfully, nothing serious had resulted, unless one counted the large area of scratched up paint that surrounded a three-foot dent in the door.

Out here, things would probably be different.

A skid like the one he had experienced would put him in a ditch, one that he would have no chance of extracting himself from without the help of a tow truck.

Could that have happened to Holly and Ethan?

Had an animal popped out onto the road and caused a skid?

If so, it must have happened somewhere even more rural than this because he doubted a car in these ditches would go uncovered for even a day.

And maybe it wasn't even a road they were on?

Getting stuck on a path that they thought was a road was always a possibility as well, though why such a thing would result in them going unseen for two weeks was beyond him, especially after what the guy at the hardware store had said about walking a mile or two in any direction. Plus they had cell phones and despite what horror movies often promoted, it was incredibly rare for them to have no service even in these rural areas. Up in the Rockies, or deep in the Amazon jungles, or out in the middle of Kalahari Desert he could see there being an issue with a phone, but here in the middle of Illinois farm country it just didn't seem likely.

Another sharp curve in the road appeared, this one going to the right.

Scott maneuvered it perfectly and then was relieved to see a long stretch of straight pavement that eventually disappeared beyond a hill. While on this, he scanned the fields on either side, eyes desperate to see a scarecrow of some kind.

Nothing caught his attention.

Sadly, he knew he wasn't scanning very well and could easily have missed something. It just wasn't possible for him to keep his eyes off the road for more than a couple seconds.

You need an observer in the passenger seat, someone who can keep a constant visual on the fields.

An image of the waitress Sophia sitting beside him appeared and brought a smile to his face.

She would probably agree to help too given the interest she had shown.

But do you really want her in the car helping, or do you have an ulterior motive?

The answer wasn't something he wanted to dwell on, so he attempted to shift his focus. This was easier said then done. Even worse, the thoughts on what they would do once the light faded from the sky and they were forced to give up the search for the day brought about a scenario of them finding a motel room.

Or maybe she would invite you back to her place.

Does she have her own place?

Chances were she was living with her parents or something, her job an attempt to secure enough money to move toward a more populated area one day.

Or maybe she likes it here just fine.

Whatever the answer it would probably be best to figure that out before planning to spend the night with her in the motel room.

Actually, it was better not to think about that unlikely scenario and focus on the task he had quested himself with.

I'll probably drive around all day and not see a –

On cue, he caught sight of something in a field to the right, something that held a position in the field that would be the proper placement for a scarecrow.

* * *

"Yeah, I remember them," the man said with a chuckle. "First time I ever had anyone come around asking about scarecrows."

Scott smiled. "That's what I figured."

"How'd the pictures turn out?"

"No one knows," Scott said, his smile fading. "No one has heard from them since they came out this way."

"Oh."

Scott waited for more, but nothing else followed. "So now I'm trying to figure out what happened."

The man nodded.

"Any idea where they would have gone after they finished here?"

He thought about that for a second and then shook his head. "Sorry."

"That's okay." Then, even though he knew it would probably be pointless, he asked, "Any farms around here that have scarecrows you'd recommend? You know, if I was in their shoes and was looking to take pictures."

Another few seconds of thought passed before the man shook his head for a second time and said, "Can't say that I could. It just isn't something I've ever really thought about and no one really talks about them during town events or anything."

Scott nodded. "That's what I figured."

An awkward silence settled.

"Well . . ." the man said after several seconds and shrugged " . . . hope you find them. Seemed like a nice couple. I'd hate to think something happened to them, especially here in our quiet little community."

"Yeah, me too," Scott said. Though sincere, he also had a feeling the man's statement was made in hopes that it would get him to move along. "Thanks for your help."

"No problem. I just wish it really was helpful."

Now it was Scott's turn to shrug. "At least I know I'm on the right track."

"There is that I suppose."

More silence.

"Thanks again," Scott said and turned to leave, but then stopped as a thought entered his mind and spun back around. "Oh, just one last thing if you don't mind."

"Yes?" A slight annoyance was present despite his attempt at concealing it.

"If someone did ask you advice on where to go around here, would there be any areas that you would suggest they steer clear of?" He was thinking about an old X-Files episode while asking this, the one with the inbred family that lived in a rundown farm that had been built during the Civil War. "A family that just isn't quite right?"

"Well now, that's a good question. Um . . . you know, there isn't anyone that I would call dangerous, but there are some folk that like to keep to themselves and have opinions about the world that just don't match up with reality."

"Do you think any of them would cause my friends harm?"

"I suppose anything is possible, though I'd be more inclined to think they'd simply tell them to get lost when it came right down to it."

Scott nodded, but then was wondering what would have happened if Holly and Ethan didn't get lost, but tried to sneak back onto the farm to take a picture – that is, if they had seen something they just couldn't pass up. "You have any addresses for me of these families, just so I can ask them if they saw my friends?"

"No, sorry."

"Okay," Scott said.

"Out of curiosity, have you talked to the police at all about this? Seems like something they should be investigating."

"It does, doesn't it, but they aren't interested."

"Have you spoken to our deputy here in town?"

"No, not yet. I figure it's just best to look into things on my own." *Though it isn't really going all that well.*

"You might want to give him a try. The big city police might not think this is worth their time, but that doesn't mean you'll get the same attitude around these parts, especially since it would be something different for them to look into."

Scott hadn't really considered this, and had to admit that the man made a good point. The law enforcement out here might be more enthusiastic with this case given how dull their daily routine typically was.

"Plus, they'd be able to get more eyes on the situation and get help from the community, which could be really helpful and produce more results than you simply picking farms at random and talking to people."

"I suppose you're right," Scott said and actually meant it. "I'll go talk to him right now and see what he suggests."

"You know where to find him?"

"I think so. Behind the old bookstore is what someone else said earlier."

"Yep. That's it." He paused for a moment. "Well, good luck."

"Thanks."

* * *

Though the downtown area was small, Scott had some trouble finding the old bookstore, mostly because it was just one of several empty storefronts that lined the way. In fact, empty storefronts seemed to be in the majority, which was sad, especially when he realized most had probably been family run Mom and Pop type places.

Thanks Obama! had been scrawled across the window of one such place, something which he figured was probably a common sentiment out here. What he wanted to know was whether or not similar things would be said four years from now if Romney managed to take office and nothing had improved?

We'll just have to wait and see, he said to himself, his mind knowing there was no real point in dwelling on this. If there was one thing he had learned during his economy classes it was that a presidential impact on things wasn't really that significant, and that it took many years – and terms – to make it or break it.

One place that wasn't empty was a bakery; the smell from within grabbing his attention and reminding him that his normal time for lunch had passed without his having eaten anything.

The hunger, however, was a simple annoyance at the moment and not something he needed to give in too. Later, once dinnertime rolled around, he would sit down with something.

Maybe see how long of a shift Sophia works on Saturdays.

As it turned out, the old bookstore was next to the bakery, a shelf within the display front the only thing that alerted him to this fact thanks to a sign that hadn't been removed letting everyone know that the next author the Mystery Reading Club would be taking a look at was Robert Gregory Browne. No titles were given, which made him wonder if the club had simply picked an author and let people decide on their own what they would read, or if part of the display was missing. Whatever the reason it didn't really matter much at this point, so he pushed it from his mind while looking for the door to the deputy's office, his heart starting to build up with the familiar anticipation that seemed to always be present when getting ready to initiate a conversation with a law enforcement professional.

How in the world does one get behind the bookstore? he

asked himself as he passed the storefront window and came upon another deserted place, this one having been a clothing store of some kind.

It took a moment, but he eventually realized the door between the two stores actually led to a hallway that then gave access to the two stores, and that chances were good that the deputy's office was beyond the bookstore side of things.

Why no sign was given was a mystery, but then again if everyone in town knew where it was he figured one was probably not needed.

He opened the door and stepped through it, a new thought occurring. Hopefully the deputy was here rather than out on a call or patrolling the streets. That would be –

"Can you hold that for me?" a voice called, startling him just as his hand let go of the door.

He tried to re-grab it, but missed, and watched as the deputy was forced to use his shoulder to catch it before it latched, a bag in one hand and a soda in the other.

"Sorry," Scott muttered.

"No harm done," the deputy said. "Were you looking for me?"

"Um . . . actually, yeah," he said, startled. *How did he know –*

It then occurred to him that the deputy office was probably the only active office within the hallway and that it wouldn't really be too difficult to deduce the reason for his presence.

"You the young man that is looking for the couple that was taking pictures of scarecrows?"

This caught him off guard as well.

The deputy noticed his look and said, "Word travels fast in these places."

"I guess so." He wondered who it was that had called and figured it was probably the aunt at the diner because the guy at the hardware store hadn't really seemed too concerned, and the farmer knew he was heading this way and wouldn't have figured a call was necessary.

The deputy held up his bag and said, "Was actually going to see if I couldn't catch up with you after a quick bite to eat, but now . . . well . . . you've saved the tax payers some serious gas money."

"I do what I can," Scott said, his level of comfort with the deputy growing quickly. "Is that from the diner down the street?"

"Sure is. Best sandwiches in town. Well, only sandwiches in town, but who would want to compete against such culinary skill, right?"

Scott shrugged and followed the deputy down the hall toward the office door.

"Hope you don't mind me eating in front of you. I ended up missing breakfast due to an incident south of here. Girl pulled out at a stop sign without seeing a truck coming down the road at about seventy miles per hour."

"Was the girl okay?"

The deputy shook his head.

Scott wasn't sure what to say after that.

"So, tell me about your friends and what, if anything, you've uncovered so far."

Scott watched as the deputy spread his food out upon the desk, hunger pains quickly developing, and began.

Jonathan

Despite having secured the bell collar, concern about the scarecrow was a constant companion as Jonathan went about his day and made it impossible to get anything done. Adding to this was the secondary concern about the young man that was looking for the girl, his frequent thoughts on this troubling scenario causing him to check the front area of the house every ten minutes or so to see if he was out there snooping around. Once that check was complete, he would go to the back of the house and squint through his bedroom window to see if the scarecrow was still on its perch.

It won't move during the day, he told himself several times.

You don't know that for sure, another part of his mind always countered.

His knowledge on scarecrows was incredibly slim and thus he had no idea what the facts on them truly were. Last time the scarecrow had attacked at night and a shotgun blast had killed it, but did that mean this one would as well? Two different scarecrows could easily mean two different possibilities. And if they really were a part of Satan's army, then anything was possible given the power that the fallen angel wielded.

Is his power as great as God's power? he had once asked his mother.

No, she had cried, shocked and seemingly fearful of his question.

Then why doesn't God just destroy him? Jonathan had continued.

A familiar lecture on how one shouldn't question God's reasoning or plan had followed. No painful punishment had been added to reinforce the lecture since this had been before Naomi's rebellion had reached it peak, yet he still remembered it. He also recalled the lack of satisfaction the lecture had granted him when contemplating the question. It seemed silly to him. If God was at war with Satan and was more powerful and wanted people to accept him rather than Satan, why allow the conflict to continue for so long?

And is Satan really behind such thoughts?

This just led him back around to the original question on why God wouldn't simply destroy him, and since he didn't want to dwell on it for hours, which could easily happen, he shook the thought away and tried to figure out something productive to do. So much work needed to be done around the house and farm, yet none of it seemed doable. The roof was a perfect example. He knew it needed to be fixed before winter, but had no idea how to go about fixing it. The same was true of the clog in the kitchen sink that made it a pain to use because anytime he ran the water he would then have to scoop it all out with a cup. Many of the lights in the house had also burned out and while getting bulbs was easy, he didn't want to risk running out of money again, thus he was just using candles from the box in the closet to conserve what little cash he still had. Plus, if the letter addressed to his parents was correct, the power would be shut off soon anyway for payment failure, so buying light bulbs would be a waste.

Frustration overwhelmed him.

If his parents hadn't gotten in that accident earlier in the year, none of this would have happened. Well, at least it wouldn't have gotten this bad this fast. Things on the farm had been in a slow decline for many years, but that had been okay since it seemed the End Times would be arriving shortly anyway. Once they had died, however, the decline had sped up since he didn't really know what to do, nor had the skills for what needed to be done. He also didn't know where the family money was. Some had been in a jar, but not all of it, and what little he had found had disappeared fast. His attempts at resupplying himself with cash from other farms had only been moderately successful, mostly because no one had been home during those moments that could tell him where it was. Only in one had he found a stash of money. It had been in a cookie jar in the kitchen, one that he had opened in hopes of actually finding some cookies after what he had felt was another failed attempt at securing some money. No cookies had been present, just four hundred and thirty six dollars, all in small crumpled bills. It had been a good find, one whose timing couldn't have been better due to the stomach-churning scenario he had been planning for the next attempt at finding money. Sadly, he would probably have to start thinking about putting that scenario to use once again if he didn't find his parents stash soon.

Will they tell me where it is? he asked himself while visualizing the horrific plan.

Once you start using the hammer they will.

Memories of helping his father slaughter a pig when he was nine filled his head, the indescribable crunch as the hammer met the tough flesh-covered skull echoing in his ears.

Would the sound be the same when he hit the man's

knuckles or would the bone within have a different crunch?

No answer arrived. Instead, his mind started to recall the squeals the pig had made as he was forced to hit it over and over again given his inability to deliver a heavy enough blow at that age. Tears had sprang forth from his eyes following the third strike along with pleas to his father to help him, but his father had only screamed at him to hit harder and act like a man.

Eventually the pig had collapsed, though it clearly wasn't dead, its legs twitching and mouth making a heavy wheezing sound. And then Jonathan had noticed the wetness around the eyes and later, once all was said and done, asked his father if the pig had been crying.

No, his father had insisted. *Animals don't cry or feel pain. God put them here for us to use and it would be cruel if He gave them the ability to understand such things.*

Though he knew his father wouldn't lie to him, he also wondered if this statement was true given how often he saw that dampness around the eyes and heard the squeals during slaughter moments, the skulls always seeming to require two to three blows no matter how hard he brought the hammer down with the first swing. It never made sense to him that those reactions were simply reflexes from the brain. What would the purpose of that be? It just didn't add up.

Now, the man would feel pain, this he knew and was counting on since it would encourage him and whoever else was around to share the location of any money they had. At the same time, he dreaded the need for such actions because he didn't like causing pain and also knew it wasn't right in the eyes of God. Well, he didn't actually know this for certain since it seemed violence was justified from time to time, especially where the Old Testament was concerned. He also knew his family had been prepared to do violence during the End Times. The question was would this violence be justified in His eyes? Was his need for money and the steps he planned on taking a part of His overall plan?

And what about the girl?

Thinking about her produced a twitch in his groin, one that gave him a desire similar to that caused by the magazines he had found in one of the houses he had broken into.

The question on whether or not this desire was a sin didn't need to be asked. Later, once he and the girl were properly wed and attempting to produce some God-fearing children, it wouldn't be, but now . . . he needed to think upon something else.

* * *

Not everyone in the Bible was properly wed in a church. The thought arrived as he was bringing up cans of food from the cellar and realized he had forgotten to bring the girl something to eat earlier in the day due to the situation with the chickens.

Following the unexpected thought was the realization that many of the figures in the early parts of the Bible hadn't been married at all, yet they obviously took part in the act of creating children. Some of them even did it with multiple women and siblings.

Times were different back then, a part of his mind pointed out.

But we're entering a period of turmoil not unlike those times, another part countered. *Things will be different.*

Images of him in bed with the girl arrived and once again brought that wonderful, yet dangerous tingle to his nether regions. Discomfort came next as the organ hardened at an angle his pants couldn't accommodate, one that required several 'reach in and shift it' moments.

What if that was her hand?

And what if she was shifting it so she could slide it into –

He tried to stop the scenario from unfolding any further, partly because he feared times hadn't changed to the point where such wantonness would be acceptable, and also because he knew even if they had reached that point, the girl would still have to be willing to engage in such acts.

Will she ever reach that point of wanting to do such things?

Bringing forth an answer to this question wasn't easy, especially when considering she might eventually give in as a way of escaping the reality of her current situation as opposed to actually wanting to be with him. Because of this, he would have to make sure he didn't make her think that was the goal of keeping her confined. It wasn't an act of persuasion but merely one of need. She had seen things that he couldn't allow her to share with others, thus she had to stay here. And since she wouldn't do it willingly, he had been forced to add chains and padlocks to the equation, ones that he would gladly remove if she decided to make a home with him.

* * *

"Sorry it's so late today," he said while setting the plate of food down. "There was an incident this morning and . . . well . . . it kept me occupied for most of the day."

No reply, not even an interested glance, his hope that the carefully worded hint about this morning's horror might finally spark a meaningful conversation quickly fading.

Just go.

You're wasting your time.

He started to turn, but then stopped, his mind suddenly wondering if he should tell her about the guy that was looking for her.

No, that'll probably spark the hostility again.

Anything is better than the continued silence.

Grass is always greener . . .

So what.

"Someone is looking for you."

Nothing.

"Some guy," he added. "Asking everyone if they saw you taking pictures."

She shifted, a couple chain links breaking the silence as they scraped together, but that was it. No response to the information was made, no questions on whom or what they had achieved thus far in their search leaving her lips.

He sighed.

Go.

This time he followed the suggestion and left the barn stall, a thought on telling her about how he was certain the scarecrow was behind the chicken coup attack being vetoed since it would make her think he was crazy.

'People will come take you away from your mommy and daddy.'

The threat had been and still was a constant companion, his fear of being taken away and forced into the hands of a godless family being one of the factors in every decision he made.

But what's the harm in telling her? She's not going anywhere.

Because she might think I'm crazy.

Saturday, September 1, 2012

Holly

That had to hurt, she said to herself while looking at the old car that sat behind the barn, its front end seemingly cut in two and folded in over itself as if the driver had slammed into a solid pole at quite a high rate of speed.

Several camera clicks followed as she snapped pictures from various angles. No thought went into the images she was capturing, her goal simply being to have something cool to share on Facebook later.

A look at the interior of the car showed that the damage wasn't isolated to the front. The dashboard was crumbled inward, as were the seats, which had been jerked forward a bit.

Blood.

It was all over the dashboard and seats, its brown dried color easily noticeable against the lightly colored fabric of the cushions.

Questions on what had happened to those inside the car entered her mind.

And why in the world would they bring it here?

With the car in such condition, she figured the owners, if they had survived, or the family, would have had the car junked. Hell, most insurance companies would have declared the car totaled with such damage.

Gravel crunched.

Holly looked up and watched as Ethan and a teenage boy came around the corner of the barn, Ethan saying something that she didn't catch.

"What?" she asked as they got closer, and then, before

Ethan could repeat himself, smiled at the boy and said, "Well hello."

"Hi," the boy said. "Um . . . he says you're looking for scarecrows?" Though the statement was directed at her, his eyes were focused on the car, a look of concern appearing.

"Um . . . yes, do you have one here?" she asked. "We saw the empty post in the other field and wondered if you may have another one someplace."

The boy hesitated, his eyes still on the car. He then took a moment to look between the two of them before saying, "We do." A smile appeared. "Would you like to see it? It's over beyond those trees." He pointed to a clump of trees in the distance, one that was probably half a mile away or more.

Excitement arrived and overshadowed everything within her mind. "That would be fantastic." She once again glanced out at the trees. "Um . . . you'll show us where it is?"

"Yes," he said. "Let me just go get a snake stick."

"A snake stick?" Ethan asked.

"Yeah. Those trees have a creek running through and the snakes like that. But don't worry, they won't bother us." With that, he hurried off around the side of the barn.

"If they're not going to bother us, why the hell does he need a snake stick?" Ethan asked.

"Maybe the stick is why they won't bother us," Holly suggested. "So . . . did his family show up or something?" She figured she would have heard a car on the gravel if this had been the case.

"No, he just came out of the house. Guess he was home all along." He shrugged.

"Kind've odd."

"Yeah, unless he was in the bathroom or something."

Another shrug.

"Yeah."

Snake stick in hand, which actually looked to be a hand-carved wooden walking cane, the teen returned.

"Ready?" Holly asked.

"Yep." He turned toward Ethan. "Is it okay if you wait by the car?"

"What?" Ethan asked.

"Oh, because of my parents. They'll be home soon and I don't want them to freak out when they see the car and no one home. Might get worried that something happened and come after us with a shotgun."

Ethan looked at Holly, face concerned, who then looked at the teen and said, "Would it be better if we all waited for them to come home so we can introduce ourselves?"

"Well, it's a bit of a walk to the scarecrow and it may start to get dark soon, especially down by the creek. And it might take them some time to get home still. They're with . . . friends."

"Ah, yeah, then we don't want to waste any time." She looked at Ethan. "You don't mind staying back here, do you?"

"Nah," he said with a shake of the head. Given the way he kept looking at the snake stick, Holly figured he was more then pleased at being able to stay behind without having to suggest it himself. "You two go have fun."

"Okay. See you in a bit."

"Oh wait a second," Ethan said. Then, looking at the boy, "What's your name, so when your parents ask I can tell them you said it was okay to be here and are taking her to the scarecrow?"

"Jonathan," the teen said without any hesitation and turned back to Holly. "Ready?"

"Yep. Let's go."

* * *

The two walked in silence for some time before Holly said, "It's such a relief that you have a scarecrow here. We've been driving all over town today looking for one for my pictures and haven't seen anything worthwhile yet."

"Not many real scarecrows on other farms," Jonathan said.

"I guess not."

The two walked a little ways in silence before Jonathan asked, "Did someone tell you about our scarecrow?"

"Nope, we just pulled up to see if you had one."

Jonathan seemed to ponder that for a moment, stick poking at the low hanging cornstalk branches as they walked.

"Why were you taking pictures of the house and car?"

"Huh?"

"I saw you taking pictures of the house from the window and then the car when we walked around." Concern was present in his voice, which caught her off guard.

"I don't know, it just seemed interesting. I like taking pictures and am in a photo class."

"Photo class?"

"Yeah, for school."

"My mom never taught me classes like that."

"Oh, did you home school?"

"What do you mean?"

"You said your mom taught you; did she teach you here at home or did you go to the local school?" Even as she asked, she knew the answer would be the former given his puzzlement at the term *home school*.

"Home."

"That's cool," she said, unsure what else to say.

"Stop!" he hissed a few steps later.

"What?"

"Shhh." He pointed with the stick beyond her into the corn. "See it?"

Holly followed the direction of the stick, her heart racing and her eyes expecting to see a snake coiled up watching them.

Whoosh!

She heard the sound just as the object cracked against the back of her head, a momentary field of blackness replacing everything around her. Within it, she saw the CRACK! in the form of yellow sparks, but wasn't really sure what to make of it.

A second blow hit and she felt herself fall, something sharp cutting into her right hand.

Don't black out! an inner voice cried, one that was unfamiliar to her.

Her surroundings came back into view and she was able to move, though her body was completely unsteady and felt on the verge of collapse.

Fighting to maintain her balance, she headed back toward the farm, her eyes just able to make out the roofline above the rows of dying corn.

Behind her she could hear Jonathan in pursuit, the cornstalks crunching as his body crashed thorough them.

"Ethan!" she attempted. "Help me!"

She had no idea if her voice was audible, or if it even carried, and felt a sudden drain of strength as her lips closed.

At the same moment something caught her feet and this time she was unable to maintain her balance.

Footsteps caught up with her.

She heard the *whoosh* and once again saw the crack of the impact within her head.

After that, everything faded.

* * *

Pain laced confusion welcomed her back into the waking world, the thinking part of her brain unable to process anything as everything around her slowly came back into focus.

Something buzzed.

Something else crawled.

Panic hit and she began to swat at everything, her face seemingly covered in all kinds of bloodthirsty critters.

The boy, Jonathan!

Ethan!

She rolled onto her side and attempted to sit up.

A series of dry heaves hit, but only a little bit of bile arrived.

Ethan screamed, his voice carried to her from a great distance.

Silence.

She stood.

The world spun.

She grabbed a cornstalk to maintain her footing and closed her eyes.

Another dry heave struck.

She spit several times in an attempt to remove the taste from her mouth without much success and then opened her eyes once again.

The world stayed still.

He moved me, she realized, the edge of the cornfield easily visible.

Ten steps and she found herself behind the barn.

Nothing was stirring.

Even the chickens were silent.

Get a weapon.

She looked at the car and then shifted her gaze over to a

junk pile, one that seemed nearly identical to the others she had caught glimpses of on all the farms they had visited.

Several weapon-like objects were available.

She grabbed a broken two by four that had nails sticking out of it and gave it a practice swing, one that nearly dropped her to her knees as her brain protested the movement.

Deep breath.

Everything stilled.

Cell phone.

Call for help.

Her pockets were empty.

No camera either.

Had he taken them or just left them somewhere in the field?

Doesn't matter.

Another shout echoed.

It came from the area in front of the barn.

Weapon in hand, Holly headed that way.

Ethan

"Ah fuck it," Ethan said after several attempts at uploading a picture of the chickens to Facebook. He also couldn't seem to post a status out here, the wireless connection to his phone too weak despite the fact that he had a pretty good phone signal.

Or the Facebook app is being a bitch again.

Both possibilities seemed plausible.

Bored, he typed up a text for Holly asking if they had reached the scarecrow yet, but then hesitated in sending it.

Don't want her to think I'm rushing them.

Given how she had been twisting and turning everything he said today, such a concern was warranted.

He put the phone away and took a stroll over to the area of corn that they had stepped into, his eyes attempting to see if he could catch a glimpse of them moving through the cornstalks toward the clump of trees.

Nothing.

He turned and walked back to the car, his mind once again going over what he would tell the parents if they arrived.

After that, he pondered how odd it was for the kid to suddenly come outside after they had been here for a while, but then reminded himself of what he had suggested to Holly about him probably having been in the bathroom.

Still, something off about him.

Something not quite right.

And yet you let him go off into the field with Holly.

Ethan thought about this for a second but then concluded that Holly had let herself go off into the field with him, and that if he had tried to go with, the kid would have probably said 'screw it' and gone back inside.

And once again, you would be blamed for ruining her project.

He shook his head and then walked over to the barn door to peek inside, his boredom getting the better of him.

A truck sat within, one that made him wonder just how many vehicles this family owned.

Was the wreaked car on the other side theirs as well?

No answer arrived.

Though he wanted to explore the inside of the barn, he knew that actually stepping beyond the doors without permission wasn't right, and returned to the car, his thinking being he might read a little more of that book from the writer guy living in DeKalb.

A high-pitched cry reached his ears, one that almost sounded like a scream.

Holly?

Nothing followed.

Unsure what to do, he sent her a text asking if she was okay and then headed back behind the barn to see if anything was amiss in the field.

No answer to his text.

Do I go after them?

What if it wasn't a scream I heard, but just some typical sound that carries across the wind from time to time?

A slide show of unnamable animals went across his mind's eye while thinking this. Whether or not a sound like what he had heard could come from any of them was beyond his ability to reason out. He simply didn't know enough about such things.

He looked at his phone even though he hadn't felt it buzz.

Still no reply.

Indecision gripped him.

Seconds turned to minutes.

Screw it, I'm going in, he decided and started toward the corn.

Footsteps stopped him.

Jonathan took shape in the corn and stepped out, his breathing heavy.

"Everything okay?" Ethan asked.

"What? Oh yeah, everything's great." He turned and waved a hand toward the field. "She's taking pictures right now. Told me she could find her way back."

Ethan nodded. "Thought I heard a scream." He added a chuckle after this even though he didn't really find it amusing.

"Ah, that happens out here. Probably was a car skidding to a halt a couple miles away. Funny how sound carries." He started walking. "Want something to drink while we wait?"

"Um . . . sure."

Jonathan motioned for him to head toward the house.

Ethan did and then, sensing something, spun back around just as Jonathan swung the snake stick at his head.

A reflexive lift of the arm prevented it from striking his face, but sent a horrible sharp crack through his elbow, one that momentarily paralyzed the entire limb.

"Fuck man!" he shouted, his voice a mix of pain and anger.

Jonathan studied him.

Ethan waited; eyes fixed on the teen, body unsure what to do.

Jonathan stepped toward him, snake stick poised for another blow.

Ethan stepped back.

I can take this little twerp, Ethan told himself. *Just gotta watch for that stick.*

He also needed to regain some feeling in his arm.

Jonathan took another step.

Ethan matched it.

Wait for him to swing and then charge into it.

Another step.

What is he waiting for?

Feeling was coming back into his arm, something that he figured the kid would not want to contend with, yet he wasn't doing anything.

We both want to be on the defensive.

We both —

Jonathan moved quickly, first to the left as if he was going to swing and then pulled his hands back and leveled them so that snake stick was like a rounded spear waiting for Ethan to crash into.

Feet skidding as he halted his rush inward, Ethan prevented himself from hitting the spear face first, and then somehow twisted a bit as Jonathan jabbed it at him, the blow having been directed at his nose.

Now! his mind cried, the command not needed as he charged into the kid, hands ready to rip his body apart.

The next thing he knew the two were on the ground, each one of them trying to subdue the other with little success.

And then the kid began to get the upper hand.

Gotta get to the car, Ethan decided, his mind acknowledging the reality that his occasional trips to the gym were no match for daily farm work routine the kid probably endured.

Unfortunately, breaking free wasn't that easy, not when the kid nearly had him pinned.

And then a knee landed in his groin, the blow somewhat dulled by a bounce against his thigh, yet still enough to knock everything but the sudden pain from his mind.

A punch came next and then his body was free.

He tried to stand and was almost on his feet when something, probably the snake stick, cracked him in the lower back.

A second impact landed while on his knees, his body fighting to maintain control.

A third blow, this one near the back of his neck, put him on the ground, an odd sense of numbness spreading throughout his body.

A forth strike earned a cry, the sound muffled somewhat by the dirt.

Tears followed.

He couldn't help it.

The next thing he knew he was being dragged by his feet, a voice saying something he couldn't process.

* * *

Jonathan dragged him to the door of the barn, the transition from patchy grass to gravel unpleasant. Once there Jonathan dropped his feet and went to open the door.

While he did this Ethan decided to make a move and grabbed a handful of gravel. Whether or not his body was up to the task he did not know, the pain and numbness still near the unbearable point, but what choice did he have. If he allowed whatever was about to unfold to proceed unchallenged then Holly and he would never leave this place.

Is Holly even alive?

The thought chilled him, his mind having not had a chance to consider such a possibility until this point.

Anger came next.

If he killed her . . .

He saw himself beating the kid's head against the ground until nothing but a handful of bloody hair remained, pieces of scalp and skull dangling from the roots.

Gotta get the jump on him though.

And hope to god the parents show up soon.

Actually, were the parents really on their way home? What if they were somewhere inside the house, or out in the field, dead, the kid having completely snapped? Such a situation could explain the condition of the house and fields.

Doesn't matter, just focus on the here and now.

Gravel in hand, he waited.

Jonathan returned to the doorway, snake stick gone, and walked up to him.

Wait for it, Ethan said.

Heart racing, adrenaline pumping, nerves standing on edge, he knew he would only get one shot at this.

Jonathan bent forward to grab his foot.

Now!

Ethan drove his foot into the kid's shin as hard as he could and then attempted to push himself upward while swinging the gravel-filled fist into his face.

Though weakened from the earlier trauma, he managed to connect his fist against the side of kid's ear and felt a satisfying *thunk* followed by a grunt of pain.

And then the knife appeared.

Whether Jonathan had had it all along, or pocketed it while in the barn was unknown. It also didn't matter. What did was the fact that it was out and pointed in his direction, the blade ready to do damage if the hand holding it decided upon such action.

It did.

Ethan tried to scramble backward as the blade came at him, but wasn't quick enough, and felt a sickening point of pressure upon his right side, one that yielded quickly and filled with warmth.

A scream echoed.

It was his.

The knife pulled free and then came at him again, this time getting him in the lower belly.

A pre diarrhea-like pain filled his gut, his small bowel squeezing as if it wanted to flush something out.

And then something did come out, something wet.

"No," he pleaded as the kid went to stab him again, his hands trying to grab the blade.

Blood oozed from his sliced up fingers, yet somehow he managed to go from grabbing the blade to grabbing the knife hand, and held firm.

Sadly, he knew the grip would not last for long, not with the pain from his stomach getting the better of him.

Movement caught his eye.

Holly!

She came around the side of the barn, hands wielding something.

Just a few seconds, Ethan told himself as he continued to hold the wrist.

Saturday, September 15, 2012

Scott

"So, you were basically cyber stalking her," Deputy Taylor said with a smile.

"What?" Scott asked, startled. "No."

"Well, okay, maybe not stalking, but certainly obsessing." He took a sip of his Coke.

Scott shrugged. "Maybe a bit."

Deputy Taylor waited.

"You know, it's hard to get a girl out of your head after being with them for so long. We pretty much saw each other everyday for two years and if for some reason something prevented us from getting together on a particular day, we'd talk on the phone and text each other. Hell, we texted each other on days that we were getting together too. Not a day went by when we weren't sending messages back and forth."

And now it has stopped.

The lack of 'buzzes' from his phone was something that still got to him despite the amount of time that had passed. When together it had been so constant that he would begin to feel awkward if nothing arrived during a two or three hour period, and now hearing a buzz was so rare that it sometimes startled him. Disappointment always followed, his hope that it would be Holly never becoming realized. In fact, he could count on one hand the amount of times she had texted him without prompting since the breakup on June second, yet even so he still held out hope that they would be reunited one day.

"I know how that is," Deputy Taylor said. "It's been two years since my divorce and I still think about her everyday and ponder the *'what ifs* and *whys.'*

Two years? Scott silently questioned, his mind wondering if he would still feel this empty that far into the future. "How long were you married?"

"Four years." A look of longing appeared on the deputy's face and for a moment he seemed to be focusing on something beyond the room.

"Wow, sorry," was all Scott could say.

Deputy Taylor nodded and then said, "But, that's life, right. When someone falls out of love or never really loved you to begin with there isn't really anything you can do. In the movies people can work to turn on a love switch and everyone lives happily ever after, but in reality this almost never happens." He chuckled. "In reality when people continue to push and push and push you call the police and get a restraining order."

Scott smiled, but then felt a fresh sense of sadness as a memory of him and Holly appeared, one where they had actually talked about how romance movies taught men that it was okay to stalk the women they fell for because love would always emerge in the end.

"Anyway, we got sidetracked. So, two weeks ago they came out here to take photos of scarecrows and no one has seen them since."

Scott nodded. They had gone over this already, but if repeating it helped the deputy focus on the situation, that was fine with him.

"You then went to the police, but they didn't feel there was enough to launch an actual investigation." He paused and checked something on the computer. "It does look like there is a BOLO though, which simply alerts officers to be on the look out for them and let them know they are missed."

Scott hadn't heard about this. "Has it yielded any results?"

"Nothing reported yet." He looked away from the screen. "Have you been in contact with her family?"

"No, just her friends." Holly's family had never been fond of him, though during their relationship they had tolerated his presence. Now, well, he had never tried to contact them given the cold reception he was sure to receive. He also had a slight fear that reminding them of his existence might make them think he had done something to Holly and Ethan. After all, a former boyfriend would make a fine suspect if foul play had occurred. "Several of them are pretty concerned too and are sure something bad happened."

"Judging from the BOLO I think the same can be said of the family. Two weeks is a long time to go without word from someone, so it is my guess they are probably starting to push the local authorities to start an investigation."

"But the lookout thing is all they've done so far?" Scott asked.

"Well, that's pretty standard in such a situation. I'm sure an investigator will also look into things, might even follow the trail you've established. They will also have the ability to look at bank records and see if there were any credit card transactions that could help pinpoint a travel route they may have taken." He shrugged. "Establishing whether or not foul play took place will be the first task for any investigator."

Scott shook his head. "They didn't elope if that is what you're suggesting."

"Oh, I'm not suggesting anything, just letting you know

what the reality of any investigation will be."

"And is that what you'll do as well?" Scott asked, a sense of time wasting growing heavy. *I could have continued looking for them if that is the case.* Whether or not he would have had much success wasn't really a factor in his mind, not when the point was to be doing something. Sitting here talking about investigation tactics was not productive and something he could have done without.

"Me? No. I think you've established a reason to be concerned and made it pretty clear that they were here and that this was the last place anyone saw them -- that we know of. What exactly I can do from this point forward is less clear. Chances are slim that an investigator from the county will do more than any other investigator, but I will talk to them. I will also make some rounds and talk to local families to see if they made an appearance anywhere."

"Okay, that's good."

"Were there any other photographs posted that day, ones that might help in establishing a location they visited?"

"Not on Holly's wall. The diner was the last one. I can't see Ethan's wall, but when I asked a friend if anything had been posted she said no." That said, he wasn't sure how much interest Beth had actually shown in looking at Ethan's wall. For the first couple of days after their disappearance people had humored him in his concern, but didn't really share it. Most didn't realize he had recognized and resented this, but he had.

"Were you blocked from his wall or was it just set as *friends only?*"

"Just friends," Scott said. "I guess he is a very private person when it comes to stuff like that."

"But not Holly?"

Scott shook his head. "Nah, she never really cared much if people could see stuff and never got all wrapped up in that privacy warning crap that always gets circulated."

Deputy Taylor nodded and then popped the last bite of sandwich into his mouth. Once that was swallowed he said, "Well, I think you've given me all I need to know about this. Will you be staying in town tonight?"

"What, oh, um, I didn't really make any arrangements. Is there a motel nearby?"

"Yep, if you go north about fifteen minutes along Brentwood you'll find one. Nice little place, old, but not really rundown and fairly priced."

"Okay."

"And let me get your number so I can keep in touch and let you know if I find anything."

"Wait, are you planning on heading out now to talk to people?" Scott asked.

"Yep, nothing else going on so I might as well get started." He hitched up his belt. "With any luck I might be able to find out something before dark."

Scott didn't reply for a moment, his hope that he would be allowed to tag along fading.

Deputy Taylor waited.

"Wouldn't it be better if I came with you?" Scott asked. "So I can help with the description and verify the car if we come across it?"

Deputy Taylor shook his head. "I have enough here to work with and will place a call if I need someone to make a positive ID."

"But . . ."

"And regulation won't allow me having you along in the car. Can't risk a civilian getting hurt if something were to happen."

Though it sounded right, Scott had a feeling there was no such regulation and that the deputy was just saying there was to keep him from tagging along. After all, it wasn't like Scott could argue it, not unless he spent some time digging up all the regulations, which would take a while and slow things down. Best to just go along with it.

"Well, I shall be off," Deputy Taylor said.

"Good luck," Scott said. "Do you have the number of the motel in case I get lost?"

"Yep, one sec."

* * *

Unsure what to do, but knowing he didn't want to go and sit around a cheap motel room for the rest of the day, Scott decided to head back to the diner to see if Sophia was still working. Hunger also played a part, but even without it, he would have still headed that way. He didn't know what, nor did he really want to admit it outright to himself, but something about Sophia had piqued his interest. Guilt about this was present given the situation that brought him here, yet it didn't override his desire to see her. He also doubted anyone would fault him for this given how long he and Holly had been separated.

Jonathan

"The best scarecrows are the ones that move," Jonathan said, words chosen carefully in an attempt to make her understand his fear. "They scare away the birds better and keep them from eating the seeds."

No reply.

"The trouble is that moving scarecrows can be dangerous given their satanic influence."

She gave him a brief, puzzled look.

"At least, that is what my grandfather always told us," he added, his thinking being that by stating this he wasn't necessarily claiming to believe such things, which might help her grow more comfortable with him. Such comfort was important for building trust, after which, once the foundation was solid, he could slowly help her understand the truth about the satanic influences in the world without fear of being rejected. "He knew a lot about such things having been brought up in a pure Christian family that hadn't been warped by the different church doctrines that have plagued our religion."

"Thou shall not kill," Holly said, surprising him. Since the beginning of her imprisonment two weeks ago, he could count on one hand the amount of times she had replied to him with an actual statement rather than simple vulgar threats that would never be realized.

"Killing without justification is a sin, of that there is no question," he agreed. "However, when justified, it is perfectly acceptable, as is evidenced throughout the

Bible."

Sex outside of marriage is also evidenced, his mind reminded him, *and sometimes no consent is given from the woman involved.*

He tried pushing the thought away, but couldn't rid himself of it fully.

"And what was the justification for killing my boyfriend?" she demanded, voice more solid sounding this time around.

"He saw too much."

"And me. Why haven't you killed me too?"

"Because I want . . ." he hesitated.

She waited, her look nearly drawing the words from him despite the fact that she was *his* captive and thus should be practicing a level of subservience.

You can't tell her why, he concluded. Doing so would just serve to make her more resistant to the possibility of being married to him later on. No. He needed to keep that to himself and allow the situation to drive itself toward that goal naturally. In time, she would grow to realize how rewarding such a step would be, but only if he didn't force it upon her.

"I didn't want to kill him," he said, mind unsure if this was the truth or a lie. "I just wanted to subdue him, and you, so you couldn't tell what you saw."

"And what, just keep us locked up until . . . what . . . forever?"

"No, until . . ." again he wasn't sure if he should tell her about how society was getting ready to crumble. Some people believed such things, especially with all the 2012 stuff coming to a head, but others thought it was all nonsense. If she was of the later category it would just help strengthen her opinion that he was crazy, if she had this opinion of him right now.

She probably does.

But that doesn't mean you have to add credibility to it.

Plus, in time, the opinion might fade and she would grow more and more inclined to understand why he had to do the things he did.

"Until what?" she asked.

"You'll see." He didn't like the answer, but it was the best he could give her at the moment.

No response followed.

You've talked enough; let her eat in peace.

He started to make good on the suggestion, but then stopped and asked, "Did you love him?"

She returned his gaze, but didn't reply.

Why he wanted to know this was a mystery, yet he did, and the lack of reply irritated him.

You could make her talk, he said to himself, but then quickly pushed the thought away.

Given the situation, he could make her do anything, but that wasn't the route he wanted to take. Nope. He wanted her actions to be chosen by her own mind without influence from him.

Several more seconds came and went without a reply, at which point he decided to leave the barn and finish up with everything he needed to do that day.

You never actually warned her about the scarecrow, he realized about thirty seconds later while stepping out onto the gravel beyond the barn door. Doing so had been his main reason for talking to her.

Nothing you could have said would have made her believe the scarecrow could cause her harm if it broke free again.

Still, it would have been a good idea to get the idea in her head just so she wouldn't be too surprised if did come for her.

But what would she do if it did?

The chain would keep her from being able to get away.
The chain would keep it from freeing her.

The last scarecrow had come for Naomi due to the love the two had shared. The same could happen here if these two had been in love.

But she wouldn't answer the question.

Why?

Would they have been out here together if they hadn't been in love?

The more he thought about it the less certain he became of everything, so he decided to clear his head of all thoughts.

Besides, you've added chains to the scarecrow, which it won't be able to break, so there is nothing to worry about.

The thought did little to calm his concern.

* * *

Thoughts on Naomi plagued him for the rest of the afternoon, his mind unable to push her away given how focused he had become on the scarecrow and his fear of an attack that night. A sense of loss accompanied his thoughts, one that eventually caused him to retrieve the photo box he had secretly put together all those years ago.

'I know it's hard, but we each need to purge ourselves of her,' his mother had said. *'Her memory and the love we each held for her is now a window that Satan can use to sneak inside us with. We don't want that to happen, do we?'*

'No,' Jonathan had said, tears falling from his eyes.

'Good, so go gather everything you have that connects you with her and burn it.'

He had done as instructed, up until the burning it part. Such a step he could not take, though he wanted to due to the fear he held of Satan and the threat his mother had warned about. Something just wouldn't let him proceed, and instead of burning all the photos of them together, and the toys and item she had given him during the years, he tucked them away for safekeeping and threw some garbage from behind the barn into the flames. Watching from inside, his parents would have seen the smoke rising up from the fire pit and assumed he had done what was necessary. At least this is what he had hoped at the time. Fear that they would discover the truth of his actions had plagued him for several months following the fire, and twice he had been on the verge of throwing out the box. Thankfully, such a discovery had never been made, nor did Satan ever use his loving memories of Naomi to enter into him.

That you know of, he now said to himself while looking at a picture of the two.

Maybe all his questioning on the teachings his parents had instilled in him was due to Satan having slithered in at some point. Maybe the death of his parents had been orchestrated by Satan to make him more accessible. Maybe . . .

He shook the thoughts away, not because he questioned the validity of such possibilities, but because he didn't think it had actually happened to him. Satan worked through people, of this he was certain, but he honestly didn't believe he was one of them. He also had his doubts that Naomi had been one as well. Influenced, yes; but completely possessed and controlled, no. After all, why use the scarecrow to torment him and, in early years, the family, if he could simply slip in unnoticed? It didn't make any sense.

He pulled another photo out of the box and looked at it. In it Naomi and he were getting ready to jump into a swimming hole the family had maintained near the creek in the north field; that was, until his father had caught Naomi and her unapproved boyfriend swimming in it late one night, naked.

Screams entered his mind, first those of his mother and father screaming at her, and then her screams as they decided to make her breasts unappealing to the men Satan wanted her to seduce, their hope being that Satan would view her body as useless and leave her be.

This hadn't been the case.

The welts and bruises across the breasts that night had not prevented anything, nor had the later more-extreme acts of disfigurement their parents had decided upon.

And then came the night of the scarecrow and the realization that nothing could ever save Naomi.

Saturday, September 1, 2012

Holly

Moving soundlessly across the gravel toward the two was not possible, so Holly charged, the splintered length of wood held high and ready to be brought down upon Jonathan's skull.

Alerted, Jonathan twisted toward her, eyes going wide, and tried to scramble away, his body tumbling as one of his legs became entangled with Ethan's.

The two rolled, Ethan's body inadvertently shielding Jonathan as he tried to get the upper hand.

"Ethan, move!" Holly screamed.

An odd sound echoed, one that was punctuated by a sickening grunt from Ethan. He then crumbled onto Jonathan, almost as if he were trying to pin him, but going about it with the inability to use his arms.

Jonathan squirmed, body trying to wiggle free. While he did this, Ethan rolled off, both hands clutching his stomach.

Blood!

Holly hadn't seen it before, but now realized it was oozing from a wound in Ethan's stomach. She then saw the knife as Jonathan scrambled back to his feet, his movements slow from exhaustion.

She swung the length of wood before he could regain his composure, a cry leaving her lips.

Jonathan dodged the swing, and then charged into her,

his shoulder crashing into her chest and knocking her backward.

Somehow she kept her grip on the wood, not that it was going to do her much good. Given the length, and the nails, it looked threatening, yet was only useful when going after a stationary, unaware target thanks to the time it took to bring it back into a swinging position.

Better than nothing, she decided while continuing to put space between her and Jonathan, hands bringing the two by four up as if she were a batter waiting for the perfect pitch.

Jonathan shifted the knife to his left hand so he could wipe the blood from his right, and then looked over at Ethan who was still on the ground.

Holly followed his gaze, eyes careful not to lose focus on Jonathan as she looked upon Ethan, who, it appeared, was attempting to get up, one hand holding his stomach while the other pushed against the ground.

He then crashed back down; face slamming into the gravel in such a way that Holly couldn't help but wince.

Jonathan returned his focus on her.

Holly looked back at him, but then, noting movement from Ethan, took another glance his way and watched as he squirmed around for several seconds, a hand in his pocket, almost as if he were searching for something.

Car keys!

The realization struck her just as he pulled them out and held them in his fist, his eyes looking at her and then at the keys.

Holly gave a slight nod; one that she hoped conveyed understanding to Ethan while also going unnoticed by Jonathan.

Whether or not this was the case, she didn't know, nor did she dwell on it. Instead, she tried to think up a way of getting around to Ethan, grabbing the keys and then getting to the car so she could drive for help.

Would it be in time to help Ethan?

How bad is his wound?

Only speculation followed, none of which was helpful, so she pushed the thoughts away and returned her focus upon Jonathan.

Knife back in his right hand, he stared her down, body giving no indication of what his next move would be.

He's waiting for you to make a move, Holly concluded, mind wondering if the two by four was having a psychological effect on him given its appearance.

Keeping a look of readiness upon her face and in her arms, Holly slowly moved herself toward Ethan, her hope being that Jonathan would think she was simply going that way to shield him rather than grab the keys.

Jonathan twisted with her as she circled, though he made no move toward her.

He's nervous, she realized, mind noting that he kept wiping sweat from his face as she backed away. Then again, she was nervous too. Terrified really. Still, noting his apprehension gave her an odd boost of confidence. Nothing was set in stone. The outcome of this was still undecided. She could get away.

Just gotta grab those keys and get into the car.

It was then that she realized Jonathan stood between her and the vehicle, which meant she would have to either run in a different direction and hope she could circle around and make it into the car before he caught up with her, or clobber him with the two by four.

Given the ease with which he had dodged her swing, she figured running was her best bet.

"Car keys," Ethan muttered once she was close.

"I know," she replied and then, hoping Jonathan had

not noticed what was said, added, "Everything's going to be okay."

Ethan didn't mention them again.

Now or never, her mind urged.

Hesitation was working its way in. She only had one real shot at this and if she fucked it up . . .

Do it!

She did, arms throwing the two by four at Jonathan with a grunt and then dropping down to grab the keys, which she actually missed on her first pass, fingers smashing into the ground.

Fuck!

The second attempt got them, both attempts occurring before the two by four even landed.

Seemingly stunned, and probably a bit confused as to why she would toss her weapon at him, Jonathan didn't give chase right away. Once he did, she was already behind the barn, feet steering her around the barn and junk heap so she could round it and get to the car.

Jonathan rounded the other side, their bodies almost colliding with each other. Thankfully, her momentum was pushing her in the direction of the car, while his had been going toward the field – probably because he thought she was heading that way in hopes of reaching the road on foot and getting help from a passing car – so she was able to achieve some distance once again as he was forced to stop and shift directions.

Even better, the car had automatic locks on it, so she didn't have to worry about missing the keyhole with the key while trying to get in, and once inside getting the key into the ignition wasn't as difficult as the movies would have made it out to be.

The engine started without a problem.

Go! Go! Go!

Tires spun as she pressed the gas, the car fishtailing from a standstill as it tried to catch hold of the surface.

Glass shattered.

Holly screamed as Jonathan reached in and tried to grab her, his hands catching her clothes and hair several times, but never able to maintain a grip as she fought back with the nails of her right hand.

And then the car lurched forward, Holly's body thumping against the seat.

Jonathan cried out and jumped back from the window.

Holly twisted the wheel and again felt the car skid slightly as she brought it back around to face the driveway. While doing this she caught sight of Ethan on the ground and wondered if she had time to stop and grab him.

No!

She heeded the inner cry and added pressure to the gas pedal, eyes shifting their focus toward the driveway that disappeared into the corn and small clump of trees.

Jonathan made one last effort to get at her, but didn't even come within three feet of reaching into the window.

In the rearview mirror, she watched as he gave chase. It was a fruitless pursuit, yet one that he looked to follow through with, which startled her.

The first of three sharp curves appeared, one that forced her to use the brakes. Thankfully, Jonathan wasn't close enough to take advantage of the slowdown. In fact, she never even saw him as the car shifted around to follow the path, tires protesting against the loose surface.

She released the brake and pressed the gas again.

Gravel sprayed.

The next curve was sharper than the first and required her to come to a near stop so she wouldn't crash into the corn.

Managing that without incident, she pressed the gas again and sped toward the final curve, an easy one that rounded the trees and would bring her face to face with the road.

The car skidded and this time she couldn't correct it in time before clipping a tree.

Jolted, but okay, she pressed the gas.

The car wobbled while continuing forward, and for a moment she wondered if she had screwed up the tire alignment.

Doesn't matter.

Just get to the road.

Once there she didn't care what problems the car presented her with, not when the possibility of being helped by someone driving by would be in play. Plus, she could always seek help from a farm family, one who could contact the police.

In time to help Ethan?

She pondered this for a second, but then shifted focus as the drainage ditch loomed, her mind having forgotten how narrow the earthen bridge spanning it was.

Her angle was wrong.

She hit the brakes.

Too late!

The front tire went over the right edge, her body thrown forward as the front end crashed into the opposite bank, and then bounced backward as the airbag slammed into her.

Fuck was all her mind could say before the darkness overwhelmed her.

Ethan

Though it didn't make the pain go away completely, Ethan did discover he was able to calm the near constant agony by staying curled in the fetal position on his right side. The only exception to this was when the gut wrenching spasms raced through him, ones that almost felt as if his intestines were systematically trying to squeeze away the damage that had been inflicted. These moments, which came without warning, always brought fresh tears to his damp eyes and caused the rest of his body to squeeze itself against the pain.

Relief always followed, an odd sense of calmness overwhelming him for a few seconds, almost as if some form of painkiller had flowed through his bloodstream and silenced everything. Movement, however, would prove this to be false, as would the dampness he could feel that slowly trickled from the two stab wounds and, at times, his butt.

He was in one of those calm moments now, the pain from the most recent spasm having faded completely.

Did she make it?

Quite a bit of time had passed since Holly's departure, a moment that had brought about a silent celebration within him.

Speculation on what would happen next arrived, an image of emergency vehicles filling his mind's eye.

They could be descending upon this place right now.
They could –
A spasm hit.

All thought fled as his body clenched, his mind only able to focus on the pain, which seemed to last for several minutes, yet was more likely only seconds.

Once it passed, he took a deep, calming breath, and then prayed that they would get there fast. One simple shot and he would be out, his body on the way to a hospital to be patched up.

Or will they just make me comfortable and wait for the inevitable?

He knew his wounds were severe, of that there was no doubt, but were they at the point where medical attention would be useless? Given the stories he had heard about things people had survived, he didn't think this would be the case, but also knew that a lot of it depended upon timing, and that with each passing second the odds of surviving something like this got worse and worse.

Unfortunately, thanks to his history class, he also knew that abdominal wounds could take a long time to die from, sometimes days. The idea of staying curled up like this for that amount of time was scary, and something he didn't want to experience.

You won't stay here for days.

One of two things would happen. Either Holly would bring medical attention to him, or the boy would return and finish him off.

Another spasm arrived, this one seemingly worse than any of the previous ones. It lasted longer too, and this time it didn't just seem that way in his head. No. Tears had time to dampen his eyes, and then flowed freely, and his teeth clenched to the point where fracture was a risk. Sweat began seeping from his pores as well, yet he didn't feel warm. In fact, a chill had arrived.

Stay conscious!

Why?

These thoughts arrived as the spasm finally started to release him, but then faded quickly. No others followed, not with the blissful sense of relief that arrived.

Footsteps appeared.

Though he knew it would bring pain, he couldn't help but shift himself a bit so he could see the source, his hope that it was a police officer or paramedic needing to be fulfilled.

No! his mind screamed.

Had it just been the boy he could have still held onto some hope that Holly would bring rescue, but this wasn't the case. Somehow, he had gotten Holly and was now carrying her lifeless body toward the barn, which he eventually disappeared into.

A huge sense of despair arrived.

No help would come.

He would die.

Holly too, if she was even still alive.

The barn doors, which had only been open a crack, were pulled all the way open from within, yet the boy did not step back through them. Instead, an engine came to life and then the truck pulled out, the boy behind the wheel.

Ethan watched as he drove down the gravel driveway and disappeared into the corn.

Questions on what he was doing started to arrive, but then were dismissed with a simple thought of *does it really matter?*

The answer was *no.*

One did arrive several minutes later, however. The boy was attempting to tow the car back toward the barn, the truck struggling every foot of the way until it finally came to a halt upon the large gravel expanse.

How much time had passed to achieve this was a mystery to Ethan. All he knew was that several spasms had come and gone during it and that the relief he had felt from being in a fetal position was no longer as great as it had been earlier.

And then Jonathan came and dragged him into the barn, a moment that caused such pain that he couldn't focus on anything else. In fact, it was so bad that his mind drifted away. He wasn't unconscious, but to say he was conscious would be a stretch. It was more like he existed without the ability to comprehend anything.

* * *

"Ethan?"

The voice came without any visual clues as to the source.

"Ethan! Wake up!"

The demand irritated him because he was awake. Pain then knocked away this irritation, pain that brought him back to a state of full consciousness as opposed to semi-consciousness, which, he quickly realized, was much more preferable.

Fetal position!

He tried to shift, but couldn't manage it. Something was keeping him upright.

Panic hit.

All he wanted was that blessed fetal position, but he couldn't get to it, not while sitting up against whatever was holding him, not while –

The spasms returned and he cried out.

Liquid filled his pants.

A taste of blood arrived causing him to gag.

"Ethan!"

It was Holly.

He vomited several times, the stomach contractions almost too much to bear. Sadly, he stayed consciousness throughout and with each second that passed became more and more aware of his surroundings.

The sheer intensity of the pain did fade somewhat, but didn't disappear completely. Once this happened he was able to process his surroundings.

"Ethan?" Holly questioned again, this time with a more subdued voice.

Ethan carefully twisted his head to the left.

Holly was sitting against a stall wall, body tightly roped up against the wooden supports to the point where she could barely move.

Her face was bloody.

"Did he hurt you?" Ethan demanded, lungs straining against his own ropes, which then caused pain to flare up in his abdomen.

"No," Holly said. "I crashed the car."

Ethan didn't reply.

"Sorry," she added.

The apology brought a smile to his face, though, given the situation, it didn't last long.

And then his gut seemed to squeeze itself.

Holly said something that didn't register. All he could focus on was the pain and the sense of coldness that was engulfing him.

Panic arrived and without warning, his body began to tremble.

He tried to calm himself by taking a deep breath, but the ropes securing his chest made this impossible, and caused the panic to grow, which then led to him trying to break free.

Something tore.

He both felt and heard it.

Warmth began spreading through his midsection, yet did little to battle away the cold that encased him.

Next, a gush of liquid raced from his butt, his cheeks unable to hold it back. A feeling of needing to vomit again arrived as well, yet didn't happen.

The trembling turned to shaking.

During all this, Holly kept trying to talk to him, but his mind could not process the words. Eventually all he heard was her crying.

And then his vision started to go, an odd fuzziness creeping in around the edges.

The pain faded, as did the sense of having control over his body. It all seemed to drift away.

He felt his head start to slump, and made an effort to keep it lifted without much success. After that, he tried to open his eyes and blink away the darkness, but it did not clear.

Nothing but a feeling of drifting into a deep dreamless sleep registered and then, even that sensation was gone.

Saturday, September 14, 2012

Scott

Not only was Sophia still working, she seemed genuinely interested in what he had learned during the day, the question being asked shortly after he had seated himself at the same booth he had been in earlier.

"Well, not much really," he admitted. "I found a farm they had visited, but the guy I talked to couldn't really offer up any suggestions on where they might have gone."

"Oh, that's too bad," Sophia said, a frown appearing.

"Yeah." He wasn't sure what else to say.

"You want something to drink?"

"Ah, yes, a Coke."

"You got it."

Scott watched her walk toward the counter, a debate within on whether or not he should ask if she wanted to help him tomorrow beginning to unfold.

She doesn't know you at all, one side said.

But she is interested, the other countered.

Sophia returned with his Coke.

"You know what the biggest problem with today was," Scott said.

"What?"

"I was all alone, which made it almost impossible to look out into the fields to see if I could spot any scarecrows."

"Oh wow, I didn't think of that." She pulled out her

order pad, but didn't make any vocal move at steering the conversation that way.

"And now the town deputy is going to face the same problem as he drives around before his shift is over. That's why I had hoped he would let me tag along with him, but I guess it was against protocol."

Sophia didn't reply.

"I think I'm going to go back out in the morning and search for them some more." He took a sip of the Coke. "I just wish I had someone to go with me to be my eyes while driving."

"Hmm, maybe you can get one of your friends to help?" she suggested.

He shook his head. "Sadly, I don't think so. None of them really took this seriously like I did, and most wouldn't be able to afford coming out this way with gas prices, and since I'm staying here tonight I really don't want to lose any time driving back and forth."

"Well that stinks."

"Yeah."

Silence settled between the two.

Scott wanted to ask her if she would tag along, but didn't want to jump the gun. He figured a seed of possibility had been planted and that it was probably best to see what developed from that.

"Did you want to order anything?" she asked after glancing around to see if she was needed elsewhere.

"I do, but I need to look for a moment."

She nodded and put the order pad away.

"Anything you would recommend?" he asked quickly before she could walk away.

She shrugged and then smiled. "That's hard to answer since I don't know what you like."

"Ah, good point. How are the burgers?"

She shrugged again. "They're burgers."

"Well, that's a plus."

She laughed. "Sorry, if I had to make a suggestion I would go with the meatloaf sandwich, but only if you like meatloaf."

"I do." He smiled. "I'll have that."

"Okay, fries, chips, mashed potatoes?"

"Fries."

"And do you want to add soup?"

"Uh . . . nah."

"Okay, perfect."

With that, she headed behind the counter to let the cook beyond the small window know what it was he had ordered. From there, she went around the diner to check on the handful of customers, moments of laughter arriving at several of the tables.

* * *

"So, do you work tomorrow?" he asked as Sophia took his plate away, nothing but crumbs and a glob of smeared Ketchup remaining.

"Yeah, just the morning though. My sister comes in for the afternoon and evening."

"Ah, excellent. I'll get to see you again for breakfast before I head out to continue my search."

"Oh, for sure."

"And hey, if you want you could help me when you get off."

"Maybe," she said with a smile. "That certainly would be more interesting than sitting at home and watching the talking heads bicker back and forth about who should be president."

"Oh, I know. At least we aren't a swing state this year."

"Tell me about it."

She might not be serious about helping you, he told

himself. Her answer was enough to hold him over until the morning, his mind knowing that pushing for a solid answer would probably tip her toward saying NO.

"Well," he said, "guess I better go find that motel before it gets dark. Don't want to get lost out in the middle of – " his phone began to vibrate.

He checked the screen and saw that it was the deputy.

"Deputy Taylor," Scott said, his words used to let Sophia know who it was. "You found something?"

"Maybe. I spoke with the former police chief and he said there was a family north of town that he would be very interested in speaking with had this situation come before him. That said, I've never had any issues with them myself, never even heard of them actually, so it might not result in anything."

"Still, it's something. Did he say why he would have wanted to speak with them?"

Deputy Taylor hesitated and then said, "I'll let you know if they have any information. I'm heading that way now."

"Oh, okay . . . thanks," Scott said, the deputy's hesitation having caught him off guard.

"Yep," the deputy said and disconnected the call.

"Good news?" Sophia asked.

"Um . . . I don't know." He paused for a second, hand still holding the phone. "He said the former police chief told him about a family he should talk to. He wouldn't say why, though, and I get the feeling something bad must have happened at some point with them."

"Like what?"

"I have no idea, but whatever it was it left an impression on the chief, which means . . ." *something bad.* "Do you remember anything big happening with a family up north when you were younger?"

"No." She shook her head. "Nothing."

"And you've lived here your entire life?"

"Yeah."

"Huh."

She stared at him for several seconds, and then twisted as someone asked for her. "Oops, be right back," she said and scurried away.

Scott continued to ponder the idea that something bad had happened with a family up north, something that had left a mark upon the former police chief yet not the town itself. *Something the chief had probably not been able to act upon despite knowing the family had done the unspeakable.*

But what would that unspeakable thing have been?

Nothing came to mind.

* * *

A sense of uselessness began to weigh heavy upon Scott once he arrived at the motel nearly an hour later, one that he attempted to distill by reminding himself that Deputy Taylor would not even have known that something could be wrong if it hadn't been for his own attempts at locating Holly and Ethan.

Still, he had thought he would accomplish more.

He had thought –

What? his mind demanded. *That you would find them chained up somewhere on a farm and rescue them, some previously unrealized Kung Fu skills appearing out of nowhere and being used to kick their captor's butt.*

He hated to admit it, even if just to himself, but his mind had been thinking along such lines. A sense of absurdity had always been present with the visualization, thankfully, but even so, it had still warped his expectations enough for him to think he would actually accomplish something once he located the town.

He looked at his phone and wondered what progress, if

any, Deputy Taylor was making. Was the family the
former chief sent him to really to blame or would that be
just a dead end? If they were to blame, what had they
done? And why?

No answers arrived, nor did a call from the deputy.

One hour turned to two hours, the phone always silent.

After three hours, he placed a call to the deputy but it
went right to voicemail.

Concern followed.

Three hours seemed way more than enough for him to
have found out if something was amiss with the family.

*Unless he decided to go back and see if he could find
something while sneaking around after dark?*

Would he do that?

Was it even legal?

If his suspicions were triggered, maybe he would do it
simply because he feared that every moment of delay was
a moment that something could happen to Holly and
Ethan.

But he would have called!

Would he really?

If anything, he would have called in backup from the
county sheriff.

*Unless he was breaking protocol by going in to investigate
things without a court order.*

But if he feared for their safety, it would be justified.

Scott was pretty sure the legal system allowed for such
things.

He still should have called.

He will.

Hoping to distract himself, Scott turned on the TV to
see if anything was on. Nothing was. After that, he
browsed the web from his phone, his finger scrolling
through all the updates on Facebook without much

interest.

During this, no call arrived.

He tried the deputy again.

Voicemail.

He left a message, one that begged the deputy to let him know what he had found even if there wasn't much to tell.

Another hour passed.

No call.

Frustration overwhelmed him, followed by a sense of dread.

What if something had happened to the deputy?

Jonathan

He was reliving the screams that Naomi had made as his parents had tried to solve the problem of her sexual misdeeds when the knock on the door reached his ears. Startled, but also thankful for the distraction from his memories, Jonathan moved to a window that would allow him to look out upon the porch, one that had a curtain blocking the glass so that people couldn't see him peeking through the small slit near the edge.

Seeing the uniform brought about a chill, one that made him wish he had been left alone with his memories. Panic arrived as well, along with questions on why the police would be here. Was it because they knew about the girl or something else?

A second knock echoed.

He didn't know what to do. If he answered, the deputy would probably ask to speak with his parents and eventually learn they were not here, which would lead to him being taken away. If he didn't answer, the deputy would start looking around and might find the car, the girl, or the graves.

Indecision gripped him.

You have to answer the door, he finally told himself.

But what if he's here to arrest me for breaking into houses!

Jonathan had no idea how anyone would have realized he was the one responsible, especially given the time that had passed since the last break in. After all, if someone had seen him and somehow known him, the police would have been here sooner.

A third knock, this one much louder than the first two, echoed.

Get the knife.

He would need it if the deputy tried to arrest him, or started asking questions that proved he was here for something that would lead to his arrest or the discovery that his parents were dead.

It's going to lead to that anyway, especially when he asks to see your parents.

Knife tucked away in his belt, Jonathan hurried back to the door and peeked out. The deputy was no longer standing at it, but instead, as he had feared, was walking around, eyes scanning things.

All she has to do is scream, he told himself, surprise that she hadn't done so already flowing through him. *Had she not heard the car pulling up?*

When younger and engaged in a misdeed, he had always been alerted to the return of his parents by the sound of the gravel being crunched by the tires. It was a sound that was impossible to hide while driving up, and thus, one she must have heard.

You didn't hear it either, he suddenly noted, eyes scanning the area in front of the house. No car was present.

Had he walked up?

Why would he do that?

Had the bridge over the drainage ditch not been fixed, he would have simply assumed that was the reason, but he had spent all last week reinforcing the sides and even added several planks of wood beneath the surface layer of dirt to help distribute the tire weight when driving over it.

He wanted to sneak up on you.

Catch you in the act.

But why and what act?

Thinking about this halted his hand on the doorknob, his mind wanting to figure out the reason before he presented himself.

Is it even concerning the girl or the break-ins?

What if he simply wants to ask about the supposed coyote incident with the chickens this morning, one that Ray might have mentioned to him at some point today?

No, the deputy would have driven all the way to the door if that had been the case. Same with if he had simply wanted to ask questions about whether or not anyone at the house had seen the boy and girl back when they were taking pictures.

He is suspicious of something and if you don't act, he is going to find the girl.

Maybe you should just go out and shoot him?

Just grab the shotgun and blast him with one of the barrels.

Unfortunately, his skill with the shotgun wasn't that great, which meant he would have to get really close without the deputy knowing so he could be sure to hit him. Such an approach was not easy, especially with the gravel and wide open areas between the house and barn.

Maybe you could lure him inside, grab the gun, and blast him.

This idea seemed more plausible.

The question was how did he lure him in? Would simply opening the door and calling to him work, or would the deputy want him to step outside?

Maybe just open the door so that his curiosity is piqued and he comes to take a look.

Once the deputy was in the doorway it would be nearly impossible to miss with the shotgun.

Thinking this was the best course of action; Jonathan retrieved the shotgun from his bedroom and placed it in the hallway leading to family room.

Once that was done, he took a deep breath, wiped his sweaty palms upon his pants, and opened the door to step out.

The deputy was at the side door to the barn. He hadn't opened it, but looked as if he was getting ready too.

"Hello there," Jonathan called. He wanted to get the deputy's attention away from the barn, but also didn't want to alert Holly to the fact that someone else was nearby.

Startled, the deputy spun around and looked at him, his right hand positioned close to his sidearm.

"Hello," the deputy replied.

Jonathan added a friendly wave, took a few steps from the porch, and said, "My apologies for not opening the door when you knocked. I was doing some work out in the field."

"I see," the deputy said, eyes seeming to grow more suspicious of him as he approached rather than relaxed. "You're the only one that's home?"

"At the moment, yes," Jonathan said, voice somehow maintaining a steady, natural sound. "Is there something I can help you with?"

"Maybe. Have you had any recent visitors out this way, college students wanting to take pictures?"

"Um . . ." he shook his head ". . . can't say that I have."

"You sure?"

Jonathan nodded. "Yeah."

"Could they have been here while you were away?

Maybe while you were at school?"

"No school on Saturdays," Jonathan said with a laugh.

"Ah, good point," the deputy said.

Jonathan waited, his mind trying to figure out if killing the deputy would actually be needed or if he could risk letting him return to his car.

His car.

Once again, the deputy's decision to park away from the house concerned him. Why would he do that? Was it standard? The only other time the police had come to the house had been a few days after the scarecrow incident and then it had been the chief. He had pulled up all the way to the door.

But maybe county deputies do it differently?

But why?

No answer followed and then the deputy said something about the hole in the roof.

"Yeah," Jonathan said after following his gaze. "We're hoping to fix that before winter comes."

"That would be wise." The deputy shifted himself to look out at the field, scanned it for a moment and then turned back to him. "By the way, what's your name?"

"Um . . . Jonathan."

"Turner? Jonathan Turner?"

Jonathan nodded.

"You had a sister named Naomi who disappeared about ten years back along with her boyfriend, correct?"

Again, Jonathan nodded.

"Any idea what happened?"

"They ran away together to live a life of sin."

"Yet, no one has ever seen or heard from them since."

Jonathan shrugged. "My parents said she was no longer family so she would have no reason to come back."

"How do you feel about that?"

Jonathan didn't know how to answer and simply stayed silent.

"You must have been pretty young when it happened."

"I was," Jonathan agreed.

"How old are you now?"

"Eighteen," he said. It was the age his parents had always told him to say should anyone ever ask.

"Really, well then you weren't too young back when it happened. Makes me wonder why no one ever talked to you about it."

The answer to that was simple; Jonathan hadn't made an appearance when the chief had shown up. The same was true when the family of the boy had arrived one evening demanding to know what had happened to their son, and when school officials had knocked on the door wanting to know if Naomi would be returning. Every time his parents had made him hide because of the fear that they would take him away.

They would have made me hide again if they had been here right now.

"Don't know," he said with a shrug. "So . . ."

"Mind if I look around a bit?"

"Um . . . why?"

"No reason, just part of my job."

"I see. Well, we'd have to wait for my parents since this is their place. Want to come inside and have something to drink. They shouldn't be much longer."

"Okay, after you." The deputy motioned him forward.

Jonathan did as instructed, his body ready to spring toward the shotgun the moment he stepped through the door.

One simple pull of the trigger . . .

A memory of watching the scarecrow's chest explode as it took a double barrel blast at point blank range entered his head.

Would this be the same?

Would the deputy's chest explode in such a way that he would have to spend hours cleaning the blood and guts from the wall, ceiling and floor?

You'll know soon enough.

Jonathan stepped through the front door and took a left.

Behind him, the deputy followed.

Wait until he's in the hallway.

Once within it, the deputy would have no way of escaping the blast.

Do I really want to do this? he asked as the footsteps echoed behind him. *Do I really have a choice?*

Both questions went unanswered.

"Right this way," Jonathan said as he rounded the corner beyond the doorway, the deputy a few feet behind him.

A second later, he was reaching for the shotgun, right hand grabbing it by the barrel and swinging it around into position as his body twisted.

The deputy rounded the corner just as the barrel leveled at him, eyes going wide as Jonathan pulled the trigger.

Sunday, September 15, 2012

Deputy Taylor

An odd *clinking* sound was the first thing he heard as his mind returned to the world, one that was difficult to register visually due to the darkness that surrounded him.

A dull ache followed.

It was located in the muscle of his lower right leg, behind the shin. Pain wasn't quite the right word for it, though that was certainly present as well. It was more of a pressure thing, along with a slight burn.

He reached across his lap to the outstretched leg, his right hand moving freely, mind noting that his left was secured to whatever he was leaning against, a ring of his own handcuffs encircling it.

Without warning, his head spun, the movement having triggered an explosion in the back of his mind. With this came the memory of being hit, a memory that actually played out as if he were watching the act from a third person vantage point rather than experiencing it himself. Experience it he had, however, an actual firework display going off in the darkness of his mind as the object slammed into him.

Shotgun butt.

Though he had no way of knowing if this were the actual item used, his mind pictured it that way, the boy coming up behind him as he kneeled on the ground clutching his leg, and smashing it into the back of his head.

The visualization made him wince.

You shot yourself.

In the fucking leg!

Thinking about this almost made him wish for death given how stupid it was, but then, after a few seconds, he scolded himself for such a thought. In fact, he was lucky to be alive.

Shouldn't have followed him inside.

You had enough to take him outside.

The boy had slipped up a few times when talking, making him almost certain that the two missing college students hadn't just been there, but that it had been their last stop that day. But then doubt on whether or not he truly had enough to detain the boy and look around had crept in so he decided to take the boy up on his offer to go inside, his hope being he would spot something even more conclusive.

Sadly, he hadn't been expecting the shotgun.

Lucky for him the shell had not gone off, the dry click of the hammer snapping him out of his frozen state of terror and allowing him to duck around the corner to grab his own gun.

And you fucking shot yourself.

Thousands upon thousands of rounds fired on the range and in the fields behind his house, all without incident, and the first time he actually had to pull the gun while on duty and he grabbed the fucking trigger.

He couldn't believe it.

It was –

Clink! Clink!

He froze, and then, when the sound did not repeat, twisted his head slowly toward the source.

The darkness would not yield.

"Hello?" he asked.

"You're awake," a female voice replied.

Though he had been certain someone was there, the reply still startled him.

"You're a cop," she added after a moment. It was not a question.

"Yeah," he said.

"Will others come?"

He thought about this for a second and decided that Chief Delevan would eventually tell people of his Turner family suspicions, which in turn would bring investigators here. The question was would it be in time. It was possible that his absences from the office could go unnoticed for a while, days even, because he lived and worked alone and people would just assume he was out on patrol if they found the house or office empty. His lack of daily reports to his superiors wouldn't really alert anyone right away either given that they had become laidback on making sure he filed them.

More like incident reports now, his mind said with a sigh. If something major happened, he filed one, if not, well . . .

"Yes," he told her in reply. It wasn't exactly a lie.

She went silent for a while and then said, "He left you some water."

"What?" he asked, not because he hadn't heard her, but because it seemed so surreal.

"It's on your right somewhere, in a plastic cup. He brought it in after he handcuffed you to the post and asked that I tell you about it when you finally woke up."

Moving slowly, he searched the area with his hand until he found the cup and, despite his concern that the kid could have done something to it, took a sip. The water tasted fine, and once a little was in his throat, he craved more. Concern on whether or not he would get a refill when needed prevented him from taking a second sip.

Then again, the girl had been kept alive for two weeks, so he must have been giving her water and food regularly.

Speaking of which, he needed to find out what had occurred during her captivity.

And find out everything you can about the kid.
The one that Chief Delevan didn't even know existed.

* * *

They spoke until the sun crested the horizon, its light eventually making its way in through all the various holes that littered the structure. Nothing earth shattering about the boy was revealed, though she did surprise him with the information that his parents were dead.

"We stumbled upon the smashed up car, which is why he attacked us I guess," she told him. "He seems to think people will come take him away if they realize his parents are dead and he's all alone."

"You know, the man who directed me here, the former chief of police, didn't mention him at all. All he told me was that the parents had lost their daughter several years ago and he always had suspicions on what exactly happened to her and the guy she was seeing." He took a sip of the water, his lips needing the moisture. "I guess the parents were extremely religious, but in a way that actually came in conflict with the local church and made the officials there weary."

Holly nodded, and, for a moment, didn't say anything, her body seemingly overwhelmed by exhaustion. A heavy sigh followed as she shifted the chain from her lap and then said, "He has spoken to me a bit about the Bible and sins and how the end is coming. Nothing too elaborate though." She sighed again. "I get the feeling there's a huge conflict within him over everything he was brought up to believe, but for some reason what he was taught still has a grip on him. And I'm certain he was abused."

"Yeah, wouldn't surprise me," he said.

"Um . . ." she started, but didn't continue right away.

He waited.

She shifted herself again, the chain always seeming to come to rest against her in a way that wasn't comfortable. Then again, how could one get comfortable when living with a chain padlocked around their midsection?

Finally, she said, "I have to use the bathroom."

"Oh." It was all he could think to say.

"We have a bedpan." She pointed, voice hinting at disgust. "He keeps it clean and everything and will probably be up to change it soon since he usually gets up early."

"Okay." Up until this point, he hadn't even considered what the bathroom situation would be, but now that he knew, dreaded the moment he would have to use it given their proximity to each other.

She did too, he could tell.

Nothing they could do about it, however.

"I won't watch," he said after a while. "I know it probably doesn't help much, but . . . well . . ." he shrugged.

"I know," she agreed. "Thanks."

Afterward, once the deed was done, shyness crept over the two and they didn't speak for what seemed like an hour, but was probably only twenty to thirty minutes. Holly was the one to break the silence, her lips asking a simple question. "What's your name?"

Surprise that he hadn't shared it already appeared, but then disappeared as he considered the situation they were in. "Nathan," he said. "Nathan Taylor."

She nodded.

The silence returned and this time wasn't broken until the boy came in with their breakfast, the two plates of food carried on a tray that looked carefully arranged to the point where a little vase with a flower wouldn't have seemed out of place. It was surreal.

The *good morning* that followed added to it.

Jonathan

Though initially upset by the shotgun misfire, Jonathan was now glad he hadn't blown the deputy away in the living room, or beaten him to death with the butt, because having him as a captive could prove useful in winning over Holly's heart. If he could show her his compassionate side, one that would be displayed in how well he cared for the man, then she might eventually come to realize he was not a bad person and even grow fond of him. It would take time, especially considering his killing of her boyfriend, but that was okay. Love like that always had a solid foundation because it went deeper than the silly physical attraction love that so many couples built their relationships upon. When two people had to learn about each other and uncover the traits that made up their true personality as opposed to the one they initially indentified, they ended up feeling closer and more bonded.

But you are physically attracted to her, he warned himself, his thoughts on being sexual with her and how nice it would be always near the surface of his mind.

But she isn't attracted to me, he countered.

You don't know that. Maybe your actions have blinded her to her desires for you, but they will resurface.

Jonathan considered this, his mind unsure how to respond to such a theory. He also wasn't sure if it was a bad thing like his mind implied. Wouldn't her attraction to him make it easier to win her over once she recognized the compassionate loving side he had?

No answer arrived, nor did he get any hint at this while delivering breakfast to the two. They didn't even thank him for the effort he put into creating the meal, which irked him a bit. He kept this to himself, however, and went about the morning duties as best he could, his mind once again wishing he had some sort of proper toilet in the barn that they could use.

Maybe move them into the house and get a chain long enough so they can walk to and from the bathroom?

The idea had considerable appeal and was something he would probably have to do no matter what once winter arrived.

Such lengths of chain would cost money, though, and unless he went ahead and raided another house, or uncovered his parents secret stash, obtaining it would be a problem.

Or maybe you could take some chain rather than money from someone?

Such an item would probably be in more abundance around farms anyway, and it would eliminate the need to venture into town, which was always a risk.

Thinking about the chain brought his mind toward the scarecrow situation and his decision to use some to secure it to the post. Nothing had happened during the night that could be associated with the scarecrow, which could mean the chain had worked. Or that the scarecrow was luring him into a false sense of security. Either way he was thankful of the peace that had settled upon the farm during the night, one that had eventually allowed him to fall asleep during the early morning hours, his fear of being attacked having waned considerably as the moment of sunrise drew near.

It could make a move tonight.

Or the night after that.

Its attack on the chicken coop was proof that it would do something eventually.

The chains.

You need to be sure.

A solid answer of whether the chains were preventing it from climbing down from the post would only arrive by him witnessing such an attempt. One of these nights he would have to spy upon the scarecrow and watch as it struggled. Until that moment, he couldn't be sure and each night would be filled with worry that it may come and that he wouldn't awaken in time to stop it.

At least you know you'll have a weapon to use.

That was another positive aspect to the misfire while trying to shoot the deputy. Had that event not occurred he may have found himself face to face with the scarecrow with a useless weapon in his hand. Such a moment would have been horrible and, given the scarecrow's probable bloodlust, deadly.

Just thinking about such a moment caused him to shiver.

Everything happens for a reason.

God has a plan.

He considered this while heading into the field to check on the scarecrow, his thinking being that maybe there would be some evidence of its struggle that he could use to reassure himself of its inability to break free.

Halfway there he remembered the deputy's leg and that he should probably check to make sure the wound was clean. He had meant to do this while delivering the breakfast, but then got distracted by the need to clean out the bedpan.

An hour or two wouldn't make much of a difference; the deputy's wound far less severe than the boyfriend's had been. Still, infection was a threat and could be just as deadly.

Up ahead he spied the top of the scarecrow, the burlap sack covering its head visible above the withered cornstalks. Several holes were present in that sack, the crows once again seemingly unafraid of the being and deciding to show their bravery by pecking away at it.

Did it hurt? he wondered.

Could the scarecrow feel pain?

It was another pointless question given that no answer would ever be presented to him, yet was one he couldn't keep himself from dwelling upon as he studied all the damage that had been done by various animals during the two-week period.

How does it even walk?

The question arrived while looking at the right foot, which had been savagely chewed upon by something, probably coyotes. Had he himself been subject to such a feasting he wouldn't be able to put pressure on the foot at all, yet just the other night the scarecrow had not only been able to put pressure upon it, but also had walked all the way to the chicken coop.

Yet a blast from a shotgun will stop it in its tracks?

Very odd.

He would never fully understand the how and why of these creatures. Logic simply didn't apply to them it seemed.

* * *

Nothing about the position of the scarecrow seemed to suggest an attempt at freeing itself from the chains, and since he was fairly certain that it wouldn't try to make a move now during the daylight while he was watching, he decided to head back to the house. Before doing this, however, he did utter a warning to the scarecrow, one that didn't project the confidence he had hoped it would when visualizing it within his head. "I could burn you, you know." *One match is all it would take.*

A few seconds later, while still eyeing the scarecrow, a thought entered his head. *And watch the dry field go up in flames.* Nowhere in his mind had he been thinking about such a disaster, which meant . . .

No, not possible!

The inner cry of denial did little to push away the sudden realization that the scarecrow had projected its voice into his head. It could communicate.

And if it can send thoughts into my head does that mean it can also hear my thoughts?

Though it would have been horrifying, he wished the scarecrow would send a YES answer into his mind, one that would put an end to the new question. It didn't.

You don't scare me, he projected to the chained up creature, his hope being that if it could read his mind it could only see the words within and not the terror that hovered around them.

With that, he started backing away, his steps slow to avoid any fallen stalks that could trip him. Such a display was not something he wanted the scarecrow to see, though now that he thought about it, he realized the scarecrow probably relished his desire of not wanting it to be seen because it would show how much fear it had over him.

Distance will help, he told himself, mind hoping it were true. Sadly, he would have no way of verifying this and if it weren't true, that would mean that the scarecrow would know everything. Any plans he made to try to stop it from getting into the house would be useless. And if it wanted to rescue Holly, which he figured would be a top priority given the goal of the previous scarecrow, then hiding her somewhere within the house would be no use.

Maybe you really should just burn it.

With the body consumed by flames there would be no threat, and truth be told, it wouldn't be much of a loss. The scarecrows his grandfather had put in place had always done a great job of keeping things away given how much they moved around on the post, but this one hadn't done that at all. Nope. It's only goal seemed to be inflicting terror upon him rather than the creatures that would destroy the crops, thus it severed no real purpose.

So, drag it somewhere safe and set it ablaze.

First things first he would have to make a pyre for it, one that would look like a trash burning pile if anyone came to investigate -- doubtful, yet always a possibility.

He would also have to make sure the deputy's car was well hidden because if someone came upon that, there would be no way to explain its presence, especially if it already looked as if he had tried to hide it, which was its current state.

Scott

Having not anticipated staying overnight in the town of Narrow Creek, Scott didn't bring his wall outlet phone charger, and thus, spent much of the early morning hours sitting in his car waiting for the phone to charge up enough to nullify the risk of it dying while he was sleeping.

Not that Deputy Taylor will actually call at two or three in the morning, Scott told himself several times while engaged in the act of waiting. *Not unless his suspicions of the place he was directed toward caused him to sneak back in the middle of the night for an investigation.*

Would such a thing happen?

Scott was no expert on law enforcement, yet even so, he had a feeling that if suspicions arose during his initial investigation the next step would be to bring in other deputies with a warrant, so that they could do everything by the book.

Unless he thought Holly was in immediate danger, her life threatened.

Such a situation would allow for the immediate entry into whatever location the law enforcement person was investigating. At least this is what Scott had come to grasp from one class of Criminal Justice during his first year in college.

Had this occurred and ended badly?
Or had he simply forgotten to call?
Scott had no answer.

* * *

"I even switched it from vibrate to ring just in case I fell asleep," Scott told Sophia an hour later. "Didn't want to risk not hearing it."

"But no call," she said, a frown distorting her face. She poured him some coffee.

"No, nothing." He sighed. "And I didn't miss anything while sleeping." He opened a sugar packet. "I was so hoping to see a MISSED CALL note on the screen when I grabbed my phone, but . . ."

"Nothing," she finished for him.

He nodded.

The moment had reminded him of those mornings shortly after the breakup with Holly, the ones where he had sent her pleading text messages throughout the night in hopes of being able to set up a time to talk and straighten things out. All night long, he would think of nothing but the phone, even with the TV distraction, his mind unable to focus on anything but the desire to get a message. At times he didn't even care if the message would be negative, a STOP TEXTING ME demand, because at least she would acknowledge him. Such a text had never arrived, however.

You would have been upset if one had.

"Have you tried calling him?" Sophia asked, her voice yanking him back to the present.

"Um . . . yeah." He nodded. "Twice. It goes right to voicemail."

"You don't think -- "

"Sophia!"

Sophia turned and saw her aunt behind the counter, her hands full of plates from the service window, which was also stacked with plates.

"Oops. Be right back." With that, she darted away.

Scott sipped his coffee and then looked at his phone; mind wondering what, if anything, could have happened during the investigation of the house the former chief had directed Deputy Taylor toward.

What was the reason for directing him there in the first place? It was a question he had speculated upon several times since learning of Deputy Taylor's plan, yet no answers ever arrived. Sophia hadn't had an answer for him either, but that didn't mean others might not know.

Have her ask her aunt when she comes back to take your order, he told himself. Though he may be relying on a cliché that was far from accurate, the aunt seemed the type that would be up on gossip, if there were any to be had.

While waiting to do that he called Deputy Taylor one more time, but like before didn't even get a ring before it went to voicemail.

* * *

"Sorry," Sophia said fifteen minutes later once things had gotten back under control with all her backed up tables. "She has no idea."

"Well, it was a long shot." *Was it really though? If something happened that was bad enough for the former chief to have suspicions it would seem the people of town should know about it as well.*

"Yeah, but at least you know that he's looking into something and that if something happened to him others will look into that." She gave a smile. "Right?"

"I suppose."

"Food okay?"

He looked down at his plate, which he had barely touched despite his hunger and the time that had passed since its arrival. "Yeah," he said. It wasn't a lie. The bites he had eaten had tasted great.

"Okay good." She looked back over her shoulder to see

if any plates had arrived in the window and then scanned the place to see if any customers were eyeing her. "Let me know if you need anything."

"I will."

She started to leave.

"Oh, hold up a second. Got a quick question."

She turned back and almost managed to mask an impatient glance before he noticed it.

"Do you, or does your aunt, know where the chief lives?"

"Oh," she said, the question catching her off guard. "Wow, um, I don't, but I'm sure she does. I'll ask."

"Thanks."

With that, he turned his attention to his breakfast, one last glance at his phone telling him no calls had come through.

* * *

The former chief of police lived out beyond the town in a house that might once have been part of a farm, yet now simply sat amid a landscape of tangled scrubland. The house itself and the surrounding yard seemed well kept, however, which felt like a good sign to him, though he wasn't sure why. The lack of a response to the doorbell and the repeated knocks that followed wasn't, especially since he had asked Sophia's aunt if the chief was a church going man, the answer being a swift NO.

What if something happened to him too?

In his mind, he pictured a scenario where the deputy went to whatever location the chief had given him, was subdued by the family and forced to tell them why he had shown up. The family had then come here to kill the chief.

Just like that old X-Files episode you kept thinking about yesterday. Could the suspicion of inbreeding within the family be the reason why the chief directed the deputy to them in the first place?

He thought about this for a while, mostly because he didn't know what else to think about. He also didn't know what to do. Deputy Taylor still wasn't answering his phone and driving around asking people if they knew anything about an odd family just didn't seem like a good idea, though he would start to do it if nothing else presented itself.

With Sophia? his mind asked.

The question went unanswered, his desire to ask her to accompany him having dwindled considerably during the nighttime hours. She wasn't to blame for this in any way; it was just a sudden lack of motivation within him. Nothing was going the way he had envisioned it when setting out the morning before, and then not hearing from Deputy Taylor had refreshed all the memories of wanting to hear from Holly after the breakup.

You're hopeless, he told himself.

No argument followed. Given the time that had passed, he should have been over Holly by now, yet for some reason he wasn't. Something about her and the way they were together before all the trouble made it impossible for him to let go. What exactly it was he did not know, nor could he adequately explain it, yet it was there.

The two of you were meant to be together.

The feelings you have are a result of some cosmic force trying to right the wrong of the breakup and set everything back into its proper place.

Though it sounded ridiculous and was something he would never admit to anyone, he actually did feel as if this could be the reason why he felt this way. At the same time, if the pressure was so great for him and was due to a cosmic force then why wasn't it affecting Holly as well?

Maybe it is, only she is better at denying it.

The thought actually gave him hope. After all, one could only deny a cosmic force for so long.

What if she's dead?

It's better than her being with someone else.

The thought came without warning and horrified him. Thankfully, he did not have time to dwell on its meaning or significance, not when a car suddenly pulled up into the driveway, its driver giving him a puzzled look.

Holly

Though she hated to admit it given that it required another to suffer alongside her, Holly was happy to have company up in the barn loft; the ability to talk with someone other than the boy refreshing in an odd way. The fact that he was a police officer also filled her with hope, mostly because she couldn't fathom how such a disappearance would go unnoticed. Soon other policemen would show up, their numbers too great for the boy to get the jump on, and once that happened the ordeal would be over.

Or would it?

She looked over at Deputy Taylor while thinking this, his body curled into the fetal position as he slept, his handcuffed forearm acting as a pillow. Hesitation had gripped him when talking about the arrival of others, the reason for which she did not know. Had it been light out at that point maybe his face would have told her why, but given the darkness she had just noticed the silence between her question on whether others would come and his eventual answer of YES.

It might not mean anything.

According to the boy, he had hit the deputy over the head with a shotgun, the impact forceful enough to knock him unconscious. Such trauma could easily cause issues later, moments of silence before answering questions being one of them as the brain took extra time in processing things. The question was would it just happen once, or multiple times, and if the latter, had she missed other moments of hesitation?

No answer arrived, nor would one given her lack of knowledge on the subject.

She shifted, her hand carefully moving the chain so that it wouldn't clink, her thinking being he could use the rest after such a harrowing ordeal.

Should he even be sleeping?

Wasn't that bad if one had a concussion?

She had no idea where the thought came from, but once it arrived, it seemed as if it was something she had heard frequently during her life despite never having suffered a concussion herself. Then again, while growing up she had always heard that tilting the head back was useful for nosebleeds until one day when Scott told her it was actually bad because one could choke on the blood. Was the same thing true here? Did everyone just think it was bad to sleep after a blow to the head, or was there really medical reasoning behind the information.

Once again, no actual answer arrived.

Maybe I should wake him just in case?

In the end she decided against this, her mind thinking there probably was no harm. Quite a bit of time had passed between the blow to his head and the moment he had fallen asleep.

Now if only she could join him.

Unfortunately, her mind was too worked up at the moment for it to be an option, despite the exhaustion she did feel from having been up most of the night. So many thoughts were coming and going, one of the most constant being Scott's involvement in all this. How he could be so persistent in finding their location from one simple photo after having been separated for several months was hard for her to comprehend. She wouldn't have done it. Hell, she probably wouldn't even have noticed he was gone without someone actually telling her about it. And to think she had come so close to unfriending him shortly after the breakup, her hope being that such an act would send a clear message to him that her decision was final and that they were not getting back together.

If you had done that he might never have been able to find this town and then . . .

She would still be alone up here, body chained to the wooden rail, mind wondering if that day would be the day when the boy gave in to his sexual desire.

Such a moment would happen, of this she was certain, she just didn't know when. She also didn't know if her attempts of using his religious upbringing to stop him would be successful. Once he reached that point . . .

She shuddered and then shifted herself once again, a slight grimace arising as the chain rubbed at a tender spot along her midsection.

Anger at the chain and the boy for putting her in such a position arrived, but then she remembered how awful the first few days had been when she had been attached to a post on the first level, body unable to move more than an inch or two. Two weeks like that would have been unimaginable and probably unendurable, at least while remaining sane.

She looked at that chain now, her eyes focusing on the padlock. The first three days of her captivity following the change of position had been spent trying to pick the lock with a hairpin, one that had finally broken after an aggressive twist against the gears within. Frustration had been a constant companion during that time, both at herself for lacking such skills and at Hollywood for making it seem like anyone could achieve freedom this way.

After that, her time had been spent trying to break the chain free of the wooden rail, but despite the crumbling structure of the barn, the rail itself was sturdy. And working the chain back and forth along the wood to saw through it wasn't possible, not with the way it had been crisscrossed around a connecting cross section of the rail. Nope. Her only chance at escape was with a key or some form of bolt cutter.

One day she had actually considered attacking the boy with the chain, the slack he allowed her enough to make a formable weapon, especially if she caught him off guard – maybe during an instigated moment of sexual contact. But then she had realized he might not keep the key on him and that such an attack could be a way of signing her own death certificate.

Still, if he does try to have sex with you . . .

She didn't complete the thought, her mind having already decided that if her attempts at convincing him it was a sin didn't work, and if he didn't give in to her suggestion of letting her use her hands on him instead (less sinful), she would try to pull a Princess Leia move and choke him to death. Better that and die then live with the memory of the rape for the rest of her days.

But now maybe the presence of the deputy will help keep his sexual desire suppressed? At least until rescue arrives.

Thinking about this brought her back around to the deputy's hesitation when agreeing that rescue would come, and now she wondered if maybe it was due to his fear that the boy would try to dispose of them and any evidence of foul play before they got to him. If they didn't move in fast enough . . .

She pushed the thought from her mind.

A yawn followed.

Having been up most of the night was finally taking its

toll on her, yet even so, she doubted she would be able to sleep if she stretched out upon the straw.

Just close your eyes for a bit.

She did, body leaning against the rail.

Within seconds, she was asleep, body somehow drifting away despite its position against the wood.

* * *

An explosion jerked her awake, the movement causing her to snap her head against the cross section of the rail, which hurt.

Another blast echoed.

"Shotgun," the deputy said.

"What?" she asked.

"He's firing a shotgun at something."

"At the police," she said, her mind picturing swarms of cops out there, a shootout taking place.

"No, I don't think so," he said after a moment. "I think he's just shooting it himself, probably testing it after yesterdays misfire."

In anticipation of the police coming, she suggested to herself. No other explanation seemed likely.

Several seconds of silence passed before two more blasts echoed. After that, more silence.

"I don't think he's found the shotgun in my trunk," Deputy Taylor said.

"How can you tell?" she asked.

"His was a double barrel, which requires loading after both barrels are fired. The one I have is pump action."

"Have you ever had to use it?" She wasn't sure why she asked it, but she did.

"Just on deer."

"You hunt!"

"No, no, deer that've been hit on the road and are suffering."

"Oh." She hadn't thought about that, but then recalled all the times she had seen them hit on Peace Road and Route 23. Always so sad and if they were suffering . . .

She shook the thought away.

Two more blasts echoed.

After that, he switched over to something smaller, probably the deputy's handgun.

"I only had three clips for it, so he probably won't fire much, not unless he has access to more."

"Hopefully not." That would make a drawn out standoff less likely should the police arrive.

"Yeah."

As expected by the deputy, only five rounds were fired before the shooting ceased completely.

"Do you think it's possible that Scott will show up here?" she asked after several minutes.

"I didn't tell him the location, but . . . if he asks around he may find himself directed this way."

Fear at what could happen to him if he came here alone filled her head. Hopefully he would wait for the police and let them handle it.

Scott

"I always try to do my shopping on Sunday mornings," the retired police chief said while handing Scott a paper bag stuffed full of boxed meals. "Less chance of running into locals who don't understand what it means to be retired."

"Oh," Scott replied, unsure what to say.

"And most of the time, the things they want me to help them with are things I wouldn't be able to do much about even if I were still carrying a badge." He shook his head and nudged the car door shut with his hip, arms loaded with bags that created a familiar glass clinking sound when shifted. "Seriously, have you ever called the police because your neighbor's dog crapped in your yard, or because a kid was kicking at your curb while waiting for the bus. Drives me crazy."

"Wow. I can imagine."

Nothing else was said as the two walked inside with the groceries, the retired chief leading the way from the garage to the kitchen.

"You can just set that over there. I'll deal with it later. You want anything to drink?"

"Um . . . no thanks, I'm okay."

The retired chief nodded and then began putting items in the fridge. While doing this he said, "So, Deputy Taylor told me about your ex and how she and her current boyfriend disappeared while taking pictures."

"Yeah," Scott confirmed.

"And you figured out that our little town of Narrow Creek was their last known location thanks to a picture on Facebook?"

"I did."

"Pretty impressive. If I was still running the department and if we actually had crimes that required investigative work on a regular basis, I would have suggested you come work for me." He pulled a beer from the fridge and then motioned to him with it. "You sure you don't want one?"

"I'm sure."

The retired chief let the fridge close. He then uncapped the bottle and took a long swig before saying, "And now you're worried because you haven't heard from the deputy and think maybe something happened when he went out to speak with the family."

Scott nodded. In the driveway when explaining why he was here, he had felt like he had jumbled everything together and that it wouldn't make any sense. Thankfully, it seemed he was mistaken on that.

"So . . . what do you think?" Scott asked after a few seconds. He had expected something more from the retired chief given his seemingly talkative nature, but then he hadn't said anything after the recap.

"His phone still off?"

Scott pulled his own phone and placed a call to check even though he was certain it would be. "Yep, right to voicemail."

"Hmm." He sipped his beer.

"And I'm pretty sure he was heading there last night, at least, that's what he said he was going to do."

"Told me the same thing." Another sip. "Truth is I was kind of expecting to hear from him as well given my interest, but figured he was probably going to wait until later in the day to let me know how it went."

"So . . . now what?" Scott asked.

He put the beer bottle to his lips and finished the last of the liquid within. "Let me make a call and see if someone can swing by his place, make sure he isn't sleeping one off or something before we get everyone all riled up."

Sleeping one off? Though he didn't really know Deputy Taylor all that well, Scott was pretty certain this wasn't the case. *You on the other hand,* his mind added while looking at the former chief, *just finished off a bottle within minutes before noon on a Sunday.* Whether or not this actually meant anything Scott couldn't say, but he wasn't thrilled with the impression it was giving him.

"Hey, Dwain, Chief Delevan here. Got a question for you if you don't mind." He listened for a moment. "Oh, sorry about that. Speaking of which, is Deputy Taylor there with you?" He put a hand over the mouthpiece. "Caught him at church." He smiled. "Middle of a prayer no less."

Scott gave a fake grin.

Chief Delevan took his hand from the phone and said, "Okay, well, he was supposed to get back to me on something and hasn't called, nor is he at the office, and his phone is going right to voicemail. You think you could get someone to check his place and see if he's there and remind him to get in touch with me?" He listened. "Okay, thanks."

"He concerned?" Scott asked.

"Didn't sound it. Probably thinks the deputy is just ignoring me for a while. He's not stupid though and will send someone to the house to check."

"How long will that take?"

Chief Delevan shrugged. "Long enough for us to go take a look at the house to see if the deputy's car is there."

"But they're sending someone," Scott said.

"Not to the Turner's place."

"Wait, you mean the family's house, the one you suggested he look at?"

"Yep." He stood up. "Let's go."

"Is that a good idea? Shouldn't the sheriff send some men there instead?"

"They won't send anyone until they know for sure that something is wrong, which they won't know for quite some time. Besides, we're just going to take a look at the farm from within the field, not actually go up and confront the family. And if the deputy's car is there, which it will be if they did something to him, then we can call the sheriff back and he'll have every deputy from the county at that place within an hour."

"Oh." It was all Scott could think to say, the course of action that was now unfolding completely different from what he had expected to unfold with this visit. "Okay."

* * *

SO, THE FORMER CHIEF AND I ARE HEADING TO THE TURNER PLACE WHEREVER THAT IS TO SEE IF THE DEPUTIES CAR IS THERE, Scott typed up in a text to Sophia. EVER HEAR OF THIS FAMILY BEFORE?

Once sent, he tucked the phone into his coat pocket, his expectations for a response in the near future slim given that she still had a couple hours before her shift ended.

The echo of a toilet flushing reached his ears followed by the groaning of pipes as the former chief washed his hands.

"Sure you don't need to use it before we leave?" Chief Delevan asked upon his return.

"I'm sure," Scott said.

"Okay, let's roll."

* * *

"Never could prove anything, but I'm certain they were abusing that poor girl," Chief Delevan said while driving. "Teachers said she had bruises on her when she was younger, but whenever they spoke to her about them she said it was from farming and calls to the parents got the same explanation. Then, once she got older, she kept coming into town every chance she got as if she never wanted to be at home and started seeing a lot of a young fellow named Tom who told friends that he was going to take her away from her family as soon as he finished school."

They came to a halt at a stop sign, but didn't continue forward for several seconds despite being the only vehicle in sight.

"This way," Chief Delevan said and quickly took a left turn. "Be best if we came up from the backside of the farm."

"Okay," Scott said, mind once again wondering if this really was such a good idea. He then realized the situation wasn't all the different from going up there with Deputy Taylor, which he had wanted to do. After all, the chief had been the *chief* a few year back, and probably still would have been the head of the department if the town hadn't been forced to disband its law enforcement team. "So, did the two run off together?"

"That's what the family says, only they didn't wait until he finished school, nor did anyone ever see or hear from them again."

"And you think the family did something?"

Chief Delevan nodded. "Sure do, but again, could never prove anything. Couldn't even get the county to issue a warrant to search the property."

"What about the guy's family?" Scott asked. "What did they think?"

"They didn't like the relationship Tom was in with the girl and tried to put an end to it, which only made it easier for the county to accept the idea that they ran away together. And then the family died in a house fire one night, which I always suspected the girl's family was responsible for, but again, no evidence ever came up to suggest foul play."

"Really? In this day and age it seems so hard to hide things like that."

"It is, but only when you have well funded and well staffed investigative teams. Out here, we could barely afford the gas required for constant patrols, let alone crime scene investigators. And since no homeowners insurance was on the property, there was no insurance company to investigate a claim."

"Wow," was all Scott could say. Never in a million years would he have ever thought that the forensic teams one always heard about in the movies, TV shows and the news were only a product of the bigger cities and surrounding suburbs.

Jonathan

Satisfied that he could handle the two firearms he was now in possession of, and that the old shotgun could still actually fire when required, Jonathan headed inside to gather up the items he would need to clean the wound on the deputy's leg. It would be his second time addressing the wound, the first having occurred shortly after he knocked the deputy unconscious. Panic had been present during that moment, though why exactly he didn't know. Killing the deputy had been his intended goal, but then, after the shotgun had failed to fire and he was able to subdue the deputy with the blow, the desire for him to be dead had quickly faded. Fortunately, the bullet had simply gone through the meat of the leg and then into the floor, and the blood, while startling at first, wasn't gushing freely like he initially thought. Even so, it would be good to change the bandage and keep it clean -- less chance of having to operate later on, which he wouldn't be good at. Heck, just thinking about having to do something like that made him queasy, as did the memories of his grandfather helping his father remove a crushed finger. The smell of burnt flesh as the finger stub had been sealed was something he would never forget. It had spread throughout the entire house, permeating everything it could, as had the echo of the one scream his father had let out.

And that was just one finger!

He couldn't imagine what removing an entire leg

would be like, though he did know he would do the operation outside if it became necessary. No sense stinking up the house again.

But what tools would I use?

The string and knife his grandfather had used wouldn't be adequate, not with the sheer volume of leg meat he would have to cut away. And then there was the bone. Using a knife on that wouldn't be possible.

I'd need a saw, one that could work its way through bone without too much trouble.

Would he even need to cut through the bone?

An image of him cutting the leg away at the knee entered his mind, one that was somehow both disturbing and fascinating, his curiosity on what exactly the inside of the leg would look like getting the better of him.

Hopefully it wouldn't come to that though, his focus on keeping the wound clean preventing an infection that would require such action.

If it does, however, you could always practice on the scarecrow.

In fact, cutting its legs off might be a good way to keep it from causing trouble.

Or would it?

Once again, his mind focused on the supernatural elements of the creature, which obviously nullified all the limitations imposed by the physical world.

Except when shot in the chest with a shotgun.

Why?

No answer arrived, nor would one. Asking questions about the scarecrow was pointless, yet something he couldn't help but do over and over again.

His earlier thoughts on burning the creature returned, as did questions on why he had even decided to put up the scarecrow in the first place.

Did you really think it would help?
Were you even thinking?
The answer was a solid no.

He had simply acted, his mind having been focused on the idea of scarecrows thanks to the girl and her desire to photograph one. Had it not been for that he probably wouldn't have bothered putting it in place.

But you have and now must live with the decision.
And it might not have even mattered.

For all he knew the boy might have become a scarecrow even without his placing him on the post. The fact that nothing like that had ever happened before didn't really matter. Given the forces at work here, anything was possible.

With that thought, he spurred himself into action and gathered up the items he had used earlier to clean the wound, and then headed to the kitchen, first to clean up the pans from breakfast – egg one going into the sink to soak, bacon one following as soon as the bacon grease was dumped into the grease jar for later uses – and then to boil some water. Once that was ready, he transferred the bubbling water to a bowl and started toward the barn, his body halfway there when he heard a distance cry from the field.

Startled, he listened for a while, but the sound did not repeat. Even so, he knew he had to go check, the sound having not been one of the standard noises he would hear during a normal day.

* * *

The paleness of the man's face was evidence of how much pain he was in, though even without such an obvious display, Jonathan would have known it to be the case. He also knew that, unlike the deputy, infection would spread quickly with this wound, the rusty teeth of the spring trap he had set the day before looking as if they had been buried all the way into the shinbone.

Breathing heavily, the man stared up at him, but didn't say a word.

Jonathan stared back, unsure what to say, and then, for a moment, looked up at the scarecrow, his mind visualizing a smile beneath the burlap sack.

This trap and the others he had set had been for it, not this man, though if the man had been intending harm, he was glad it had caught him. Even so, he didn't like that the scarecrow now knew about the traps, his hope having been it would get caught in one during the night should it decide to approach the house.

It probably knew about them anyway if it could read your mind while setting them.

No reply from the scarecrow entered his head, which only made things difficult, which was probably why the scarecrow didn't reply. It didn't want him to know for certain whether or not it could read his mind.

Or it can't.

But what about earlier?

The question stuck in his head, all while he contemplated what it was he needed to do about the man before him, one who was trying to pry the teeth from his leg without success.

"Who are you?" Jonathan asked.

No reply, though he did grunt with pain as his hands released their grip on the trap, the tiny amount of movement he had generated causing him pain as the teeth returned to their original spots in the bone.

"If you want me to free you and patch up that leg you have to tell me who you are and what you're doing here."

Nothing.

"Very well," Jonathan said and started to walk away.

"Wait!" the man cried.

Jonathan stepped back up to the man, eyes trying not to stare at the imbedded teeth, yet finding it difficult to focus elsewhere.

"Who are you?" the man asked.

This caught Jonathan off guard and without really thinking he said, "Jonathan Turner. This is my family's farm." He waited a second. "Who are you?"

"Chief Delevan."

Chief! Panic arrived.

"What are you doing out here?" Jonathan asked, voice somehow able to maintain a level of calmness despite the renewed fear.

Nothing.

"What are you doing out here?" Jonathan repeated.

"Investigating the . . ." his teeth clenched for a moment and sweat started to break out along his forehead ". . . ah shit man, get this fucking thing off!"

"Investigating what!" Jonathan demanded, ignoring the plea.

"Oh God!" he cried, hands reaching for the trap once more. "It hurts!"

Jonathan kicked at his hands, the toe of his boot crushing his fingers against the trap, which dug in further.

"Jesus Christ!"

Hearing this, his anger spiked and he nearly kicked the man again, but then somehow managed to control himself, an inner statement about how he needed to know what it was the man was investigating and whether or not others were coming arriving.

"Tell me what you're investigating and I will open the trap."

The man took a deep breath. "The disappearance of Deputy Taylor." A loud groan followed and then he was once again reaching for the teeth.

"Just you?" Jonathan asked, fear that others might be on their way arriving.

"Yes. Jesus. Just me. *Fuck!* Get this thing off! PLEASE!"

Rather than do that Jonathan leaned in and cut the man's throat, his actions spurred by the fact that he just didn't have the resources or the patience to care for a third person. Plus he knew the wound would go bad fast and that the path to such a death would be painful, so really this was a mercy killing.

Blood spurted three times as the man gasped, each spurt growing less forceful as the pumping slowed. Jonathan had made sure to open the airway with the cut so that death would be quick. No sense making the man suffer more than needed.

Once that was done and the man was still, Jonathan went in search of his car keys, his thinking being he must have parked alongside the field somewhere and walked in.

Sure enough, a set of keys was there.

He also took his wallet and cell phone, eyes hoping to see some money he could use in the former. Twenty dollars was present, which more than doubled the money he currently had in his possession, so that was a good find. The badge also interested him, mostly because he knew the town had done away with the police department given things his parents had said.

Why would he still carry it?

Was he still acting as a law enforcement official?

What if he was investigating the missing deputy for the sheriff's department who would now grow even more upset over this disappearance and send more people?

No, he had said he was alone.

But how had he known the deputy was here?

This question, more than anything else, plagued him as he hurried back to the house to get the truck.

Scott

"Sorry, couldn't reply to your text while working, but now I'm off," Sophia said.

"Oh, that's okay," Scott said. He was sitting in the passenger seat of Chief Delevan's car, waiting for his return. "I figured you were busy, but just wanted you to know what I was doing in case I couldn't let you know later on."

"That's cool. So, you're at the place right now where the deputy went last night. Find anything?"

"I guess, at least this is where the chief said he sent him. I'm actually sitting in the car on the side of the road while he takes a look at the house to see if he can see anything unusual."

"Still?" Sophia asked. "How long have you been there?"

"Um . . . since I texted you I guess." He looked over at the corn, eyes hoping to see the man emerging from it. "To tell you the truth I didn't realize it was going to take this long, but I guess he wanted to circle the farm so he could see if the deputy's car was stashed anywhere or see anything else that was suspicious."

"Why not just call the sheriff's department and have them take a look?"

"He called asking them about the deputy and whether or not he was around, but didn't want to tell them about this place until we knew for sure if something was wrong and if the deputy was actually unaccounted for."

"Okay, no offense, but that seems a little hokey."

"Yeah, well, I figured he might know what he's doing given he used to be the chief and all, but . . ." he thought about the beer ". . . well, we shall see if he comes up with anything. I'm guessing he should be back soon."

"What if he isn't?"

"What?" he asked, the question catching him off guard.

"Think about it, your ex and her boyfriend go up there and disappear. A deputy goes up there and disappears. And now you two have gone up there and he hasn't come back yet after what, two hours?"

Scott didn't want to counter her statement, but had to point out that they really didn't know for certain if Holly, Ethan, and Deputy Taylor had actually met with foul play at this location.

"But you have reason to suspect it, and that should be enough for the sheriff to take seriously," Sophia said. "That's what they're there for, isn't it, to investigate things and, if possible, prevent future crimes from happening."

"Yeah, I would have to agree with that." A second later, he changed the subject and said, "Hey, did you ever hear about a family burning to death several years ago on their farm one night?"

"You mean the Parker family?"

"Um . . . maybe? Is that the only family that died in a house fire and did they have a son named Tom that disappeared?"

"I don't know about the son named Tom, but I remember the fire. It was like ten years ago while I was still in grade school. We had an assembly a few days later where they taught us fire safety things."

"Was there ever any rumor that this family started that

fire?"

"Huh, I don't remember anything like that, just that it was a house fire that killed the family, but I was nine and not really paying much attention to what the grown ups were talking about."

Silence settled.

"So . . ." Sophia said after about thirty seconds ". . . he's still not back?"

"Nope, and I have to admit, I'm growing pretty restless." Nothing was happening. For a little over two hours he had sat in the front seat, car parked along the cornfield, his back to wherever it was that the Turner house was located. Only one car had driven by during this time, its driver seemingly unconcerned about the car parked alongside the road, which surprised him given the small town friendliness he had always heard about. "If I had known it would take this long to check things out I would have . . . well, I don't know, but I didn't think I'd be sitting here all this time, that's for sure."

"Want me to come keep you company?" she asked. "I have nothing going on."

"Oh . . . um . . . I'd say yes, but what if he comes back while you're on your way? I'd hate for you to drive out here for nothing."

"If that happens just call me and let me know and I can meet you somewhere."

She is interested, Scott said to himself, somewhat startled. "Oh, okay, that'll work."

"Great. See you soon."

"Yep." With that, the call ended.

Concern followed, though he wasn't sure why.

Yesterday you were hoping she'd say yes to your inquiry on whether or not she wanted to help you, and now you are fretting over her joining in. What is wrong with you?

The answer, which he knew was absurd, was Holly. He still wasn't over her and for some reason felt as if having Sophia joining in would be a form of betrayal even though they weren't together.

She might not even be alive.

And it's not like Sophia is coming here to fuck you and even if she was it would be perfectly okay.

Sadly, he knew he would regret such action down the road if Holly and he did get back together, which he had continued to harbor hope for despite how much time had passed. Such thoughts had actually kept him from having sex with another girl a month earlier, one that had been pretty much begging for his cock yet now hated him because he had gone so far as to bring her home with the intention of going through with it until she started undoing his pants.

Panic filled 'what ifs' had bombarded him as her hands slipped beneath the waistband of his boxers, the worst of which had him visualizing Holly appearing at his door the next day with a desire to try again, only to find him with a new girl, the chance at reuniting ruined.

He sighed and then twisted around to look at the field once again, eyes hoping, but failing to see the chief emerging from the corn.

* * *

Ten minutes later Scott was out of the car pacing a narrow strip of land near the corn, his steps upon the parched earth creating a small dust cloud that shadowed his movements until a gust of wind forced it across the road.

With the wind came the sound of an engine, which stopped his pacing and caused him to look eastward.

A truck was heading his way.

He watched it, eyes expecting it to pass on by like the

previous one had, but instead it started to slow as it neared the car, the driver looking toward him with curiosity.

Scott took a few steps toward the truck as it came to a stop, its gears protesting.

"Everything okay?" the driver asked through the open passenger window.

"Yeah," Scott said. "Just had to get out and stretch the legs a bit."

"Oh." The driver looked around for a moment then returned his gaze. "Is it just you?"

"Um . . ." Scott started, the question seeming odd to him though he wasn't sure why. "Yeah, just me."

"I see." The driver started to shift in his seat, but then stopped as his eyes seemed to catch something in the mirror and twisted around to look at the road behind him.

Using the moment of distraction, Scott took a couple steps forward and glanced into the truck cab, his suspicion that something wasn't quite right being confirmed when he saw a shotgun sitting across the seat, the barrels pointed at the passenger door -- *pointed at him.*

And then the driver was looking at him, eyes quickly following his gaze down toward the shotgun. Hesitation seemed to grip both of them, one that was finally broken as Scott stepped away from the door and the driver hit the gas.

It was only then that Scott realized a tiny car was closing the gap on the road, its driver eventually bringing it to a halt where the truck had been.

"You're still here," Sophia said with a smile.

"Um . . . yeah," Scott replied, eyes turning to watch as the truck disappeared down the road, mind wondering what the driver's intention had been. "I am." *And had you been a few seconds later that might not have been the case.*

Legs weakening, he sought the car for support, his movements attempting to, but failing to look casual.

"What is it?" she asked while stepping from the car. "Are you okay?"

"Fine," he muttered. "Just got lightheaded there for a second. I need . . ." *need what?* He didn't know.

"Water," Sophia said. It was not a question, but a statement.

"Yes," he nearly cried, only now realizing how thirsty he was after having sat for two hours without anything to drink. It also was a valid reason for his sudden weariness, which was good, because he didn't want to say anything about the shotgun or his fear that the driver had been shifting around to grab it and use it.

But why?

Was he a member of the Turner family?

If so that meant something had probably happened to Chief Delevan and he had told the family he wasn't alone.

But would he have really shot me right here in broad daylight?

Why not, the road has been mostly deserted all day.

Despite the heat, a sudden chill enveloped him and brought about a shiver.

Jonathan

He watched from a distance as the boy and girl talked with each other on the side of the road, questions on who they were and why they were here filling his head.

Is that even the chief's car?

If not, he had no idea where the chief had parked because after driving away from these two he had gone as far as the road could take him alongside the farm field and not seen another one. The location was also perfect for where the chief ended up, the path from here to the house one that would take him right up to the scarecrow, or at least close enough to catch sight of it and go in for a closer look.

But he said he was alone.

Had he lied?

Such a possibility seemed likely and brought about a considerable amount of anger. Adding to it was the frustration of the girl's timing. It had been way too perfect, almost as if it had been orchestrated so that he wouldn't do something to the boy.

Would you have really shot him?

The thought had been present while staring at him, his fear that he was somehow partnered with the chief impossible to ignore. But then the girl had appeared.

Had it really been planned out or was it just a nasty coincidence?

Was it possible that God had no interest in any of this whatsoever and everything had happened just because that's the way things fell into place?

The latter possibility worried him because if God wasn't coordinating things to serve a certain purpose it meant he was vulnerable.

And that everything has been for naught.

But at least you wouldn't have to worry about sinning.

The thought chilled him to the core, yet also carried with it an appeal he couldn't deny.

Caution followed. Just because the possibility existed that God wasn't playing an active role in these events didn't mean he wasn't still keeping a record of one's actions from up above. He also had to remember that God's hand probably wasn't the only hand playing a part in the way things unfolded. The devil was there as well, the scarecrow activity during the night proof of this. The girl's arrival could have been his doing, only his manipulation of the events wasn't as precise as God's was. If it were, then the girl would have arrived moments after he had shot the boy and screwed everything up. In fact, God's hand may have acted to prevent that, which was why she arrived at the time she did.

He sighed.

Standing by the car, the two continued to talk.

The question on who they were once again entered his head.

No answer followed.

Not long after that, the two got into the girl's car and drove away, the young man having first written what appeared to be a note and leaving it within the car.

For Chief Delevan? Letting him know he had left with the girl and not to worry?

This seemed the most likely, yet once again brought up the fact that the chief had lied to him. He hadn't been alone. What was worse was he couldn't do anything about it. The chief was dead; his body still sprawled out upon the ground near the scarecrow. Any actions he took against the chief as a way to make him pay for the lie would be silly.

Why had the boy stayed in the car?

Why not come and search the farm with the chief?

Who is he?

The first two questions drifted away as the speculation about the second one arrived. Yesterday both Ray and the deputy had mentioned a young man coming to town to try to find Holly. Could this be him?

The more he considered it, the more likely it seemed, the only question now being how in the world he had tracked everything down to him. And why was the former chief involved? Had the young man sought him out? And what about the deputy? Had the young man sent him to the farm and then gotten the chief when he never returned?

How would he even know about the chief?

Wouldn't it be more likely he would have gotten the sheriff?

Or maybe the sheriff had put him in touch with the chief?

So many questions with too few answers. He needed to confront the boy.

Or make the deputy talk.

Once again, the image of the hammer entered his mind. Sadly, using that would upset Holly and probably make it so she would never be able to trust him. That said, he needed some answers, especially since within those answers could be information that might make it possible for them to stay together.

Up ahead he watched as the two drove, the girl's car quickly disappearing as it took a right at the intersection. A debate on whether or not he should follow them entered his mind for a bit, but he decided that doing so would be a bad idea given how easy it would be for them to spot his truck on these empty back roads. Plus, if the young man was from out of town then chances were he was staying at the motel, which wasn't far. One simple trip there after he got rid of the chief's car, which he needed to do just in case anyone came to check it out, and the young man would no longer be a problem.

* * *

Now what? he asked himself once he was inside the car, his mind drawing a blank on how to dispose of it. *You also need to get rid of the deputy's car, and the college kids' car.*

The latter two were in the barn, and while he could easily fit this third car within, the location was not ideal, not when the sheriff might show up and look inside.

Heck, just having his parents' car around was not ideal, which was why he had always planned to sink it in the pond after the corn harvest. Until then he couldn't exactly get the car to the pound, not with all the cornstalks standing in his way. He also didn't want to cut a path to it because it would look suspicious if anyone should arrive to investigate.

An idea appeared, but then was vetoed given the amount of time it would take to get all the cars to the location, all due to the fact that he would have to walk back after each trip.

Unless I somehow get the deputy to drive the truck behind me?

An image of putting Holly in some sort of peril that would require their return at a certain time entered his head; his thinking being the deputy wouldn't want to risk pulling a fast one because it would result in her death.

Unfortunately, he didn't like the risk to the girl that such a situation would carry with it; especially since he had a feeling the deputy would try something.

In the end, he decided to simply drive this car onto the other side of the farm and park it along a rural stretch of road by the river. That way if anyone came to look at the farm they wouldn't find the car there. Better yet, he could probably find an overgrown patch near the river to drive it into so that it wouldn't be easily seen from the road.

After that, if the sheriff still hadn't shown up, he could do the same with the deputy's car.

Or . . . his mind started as a different, better idea formed, one that would still require him to dispose of a car, but at least it wouldn't be one as recognizable as the deputy's car. Having that in the weeds by the river would draw attention to the farm in a way that this car or the young man's car wouldn't, though, those would draw some attention as well if discovered.

*   *   *

Though he knew time might not be on his side, Jonathan did a search of the car after driving it into the overgrowth, his foot bringing the pedal nearly to the floor so he could really get it in there. Nothing within was helpful, though he did pocket the note the boy had left since it had the hotel name and room number on it, as well as his cell phone number.

With that secure, he crossed the road, hopped the dry creek bed, climbed up the slope that marked the beginning of the farm and began the long walk back to where the truck was parked. While on this journey, feet moving as quickly as they could without actually running, he contemplated the action he felt was needed against the boy and further wondered if he would now have to do something about the girl.

All because two college kids wanted to see a scarecrow and stumbled upon the car, he said with a mental sigh.

Would they have even said anything about the car or just

gone on their way once they found out no scarecrow was
around?

According to his parents, people were always out to get
them, their jealousy at the family's salvation and purpose
in the eyes of the Lord causing hatred within them that
was too great to ignore. He, however, had seen very little
evidence of this during the last year and sometimes
wondered if it was true.

Holly

"No one is going to come, are they," Holly said. "If they were, they would have been here by now."

Deputy Taylor looked down for a while and then finally said, "I never told the department what I was doing because it was just supposed to be a quick stop on my way home." He sighed. "I just wanted to check things out and see if anything was amiss."

"So no one knows where to look now that you're missing too." Her voice was bitter, not toward him, but toward the entire situation.

"Chief Delevan knows I was going to be heading this way and asked me to let him know what I found."

"Do you think he'll report you missing when you don't get back to him?" *Or will he think you just blew him off?* Why her mind went this way she didn't know, but she couldn't help but picture the deputy agreeing to give him an update simply because it was the polite thing to say when asked, which in turn would lead the chief to thinking the failure to give such an update was nothing more then him being blown off.

"I don't know."

Frustration began to build within her after that, mostly because she couldn't believe how easy it would be for them to be discovered. One simple phone call was all it would take. And the response to the phone call wouldn't have to be one of swooping in with a dozen deputies. Just one would do the trick, their presence enough to set the boy off, his fears so great he would do something stupid. After that, the sheriff's department would know something was up and would send in more deputies.

"Do you think Scott will contact anyone?" she asked, her mind not liking the direction of her previous thought, not when it was showing promise with what could possibly result in another person being harmed. "I'm sure he is waiting for you to let him know what you found and probably getting worried."

"Maybe, only I never told him where I was going. I didn't want him to show up himself. He seemed the type to do something like that."

"Yeah, he is," she said. "Always was very persistent, almost to the point of being obsessive." A memory of him working on a puzzle arrived. Hanging out with him at his apartment had been very trying during that period because he couldn't leave the stupid thing alone, its state of incompleteness bugging him. At one point, she had almost swept the puzzle off the table, her frustration at his lack of attention to what she had been saying too much.

"That could be a good thing right now," he muttered.

"I know; I hope he – " she stopped as the barn door opened, the hinges squealing. The sound of the boy climbing the ladder followed, the echo of aged wood groaning under his weight causing her body to shudder.

Jonathan looked at both of them, his appearance somewhat haggard, and then turned to the deputy. "I need your clothes." He handed over the handcuff key while saying this, his other hand aiming the pistol at the deputy's stomach.

Seeing the key, Holly realized this might be a chance to attack, the only problem being the distance between her and the boy. It wasn't an unreachable distance, not with the amount of chain slack she had been given, but he would notice her approach long before she was close enough to do any good.

Shit, just standing up will grab his attention.

"My clothes?" Deputy Taylor asked. "Why?"

Don't argue with him, just start stripping, Holly pleaded, her thinking being his movement might shield her own, especially when the boy would be focused on the unrestrained deputy.

"I need them," Jonathan said.

"What for?"

Growing agitated, Jonathan cocked the hammer back on the handgun. "Don't make this hard."

"Do you want me to take off my clothes too?" Holly asked while standing, the question nothing more than an excuse to get up without having to do it quietly.

"W-what?" he stammered, head turned toward her.

"I'm guessing you'll want mine as well if you're making us get naked." With that, she began to take off her shirt, the soiled fabric feeling as if it were peeling itself away from her skin.

His eyes went wide. "No, I just need -- "

Deputy Taylor's heel connected with the boy's knee causing it to twist around at a horrible angle, his body dropping down as his weight was no longer supported.

Holly lunged, chain in her hands like a garrote wire while Deputy Taylor went for the gun.

The two connected before Holly could close the distance, bodies entangling with one another as the struggle for the gun began.

A blast echoed.

Holly froze.

For a second, all was still, and then Deputy Taylor tried to stand, an odd gurgling sound leaving his mouth, only . .
.

Holly couldn't help but gasp at the sight. The bottom of the deputy's jaw was completely gone, his tongue actually flopping between his fingers as he tried to hold things in place. And there was blood. It came out in spurts amid the jagged edges of bone, the whiteness momentarily gleaming in a single beam of sunlight before being stained red.

One such spurt caught the boy who, until then, was simply staring at the grotesque display. A shriek followed, as did a frantic scramble backward, his body crashing into her legs.

Do it! Holly's mind cried.

She brought the chain down around his throat, and pulled, a sudden wheeze like gasp mixing with the sounds Deputy Taylor was still making.

Fingernails dug into her hands and wrists as Jonathan struggled, skin easily parting beneath the chewed edges. He then reached for the gun, which had fallen at some point, his fingers inches away from securing it.

"NO!" she screamed while yanking him backward, hands using all the strength they could muster.

His body lifted and then crashed back down, a pathetic airless cry leaving his lips.

Something caught her foot.

FUCK! her mind cried as her balance failed, hands fighting to maintain their grip on the chain, which was digging into her palms.

It was no use.

The angle of the fall forced her right hand to relax and the next thing she knew, Jonathan was slipping free from the chain, all while her elbow connected with something that numbed the entire arm.

Had it not been for the numbing, she might have been able to regain the upper hand while he sat there sucking in air, but between the chain that had entangled her foot and her inability to put pressure on her dominant arm, the moment to act slipped away.

And then he had the chain and yanked her toward him, the raw skin around her hips finally tearing as her body flopped forward, breasts somewhat slowing her momentum as she crashed into the wood, which probably helped keep her teeth from shattering as her jaw snapped shut.

Pain exploded in her side, ribs seeming to bend inward as his booted foot drove into her.

A second kick landed as well, this one cushioned by her boob.

Tears sprang from her eyes as she tried to brace herself for a third blow that never arrived. Not that it was needed. She could barely move, let alone attempt another attack. It just was not possible. The pain was too much, as was the numbness that had spread into several areas.

Breathing heavily, Jonathan stood over her. She twisted a bit to look at him, a wince escaping, and watched as he turned from her to check on Deputy Taylor who was crumbled near the edge of the loft, body motionless.

The gun.

It was sitting about three feet in front of her, just out of reach.

Just try, a part of her mind urged.

Can't, another countered.

Do it!

Gritting her teeth, she pushed herself to her knees and slowly crawled toward the gun, eyes going from it to the boy who was fixated on the deputy.

Hope began to build once more, though the pain each inch of movement caused kept it from surging.

You won't make it.

He is going to see you.

The latter was true, only she had reached the gun by that point and was lifting it toward him, mind trying to steady the shake in her arm so she could take aim.

Jonathan's eyes went wide and his face paled.

She pulled the trigger.

Scott

"All I can offer is some change for a soda from the machine by the office," Scott said.

"That works," Sophia said. "Um . . . how much is it?"

"A dollar."

"Okay. You want anything?"

"No, I'll stick with the water." He jiggled the bottle she had given him.

"You feeling better?" she asked.

"Yeah." Body wise, it wasn't a lie. The water had helped combat the growing dehydration quicker than he had expected, though he had cramped up a bit after the first chug, which hurt. Mentally, however, he was a mess. He had no idea what to do. A call to the sheriff department had gotten him a promise of a call back from the sheriff once he could be reached, a statement about them being in the process of locating Deputy Taylor's whereabouts given but not detailed. Hearing that, he had tried to suggest they go to the Turner household, and had shared his concern that something had happened to Chief Delevan there.

"We will send a deputy out to the house to talk to the Turner family and find out if the former chief has been there," the operator had assured him.

"But what if something happened to him there," Scott asked. "I don't think they are going to be very forthcoming."

"Sir, our deputy will assess the situation upon his

arrival. In the meantime, I ask that you not have any contact with the family or venture onto their property. These fields can be dangerous, especially during harvest time, and it can be difficult for a worker to see someone in the field below while operating machinery."

"Okay," Scott said, mind realizing the conversation wasn't going to go anywhere beyond this. "Please keep me posted on what happens."

The operator humored him with a statement about updating him later, and then ended the call. That had been fifteen minutes earlier while the two had been making the turn from Brentwood into the motel parking lot. No call back from the sheriff had arrived, though, honestly, he hadn't thought one would for some time yet. Still, he was anxious, and didn't like the idea of sitting around. If he did, he wouldn't have bothered coming out here in the first place. Thankfully, he wasn't alone. Having Sophia with him, even with the awkwardness brought about given how little they actually knew each other, was helpful.

"I'm back," Sophia said as she opened the door, a Mountain Dew in her hand. "He call yet?"

"No. Probably won't for like three hours or something." He sighed and set the phone on the bed. "I have the feeling he was just humoring the chief earlier when he said they would investigate. I got a sense the two might have history that isn't all that great, so I'm sure the last thing the sheriff wants to do is verify the chief's concerns, especially if it seems like he's stepping on his toes."

"I don't know," she said. "I'm sure they really are looking into Deputy Taylor's whereabouts. A missing deputy is a pretty big deal even out here. And then they'll check out the Turner's farm for your ex and her boyfriend."

"I hope so," he said.

"They will."

"The problem is there isn't much to go on. I mean, the only reason the chief thinks it could be the Turner family is because of an incident that happened ten years ago. If more had happened since then I could see the sheriff being more interested in all this, but with just one incident involving more speculation than evidence, I'm guessing he is asking why they would do something to two college kids that just wanted to take pictures, especially if their name has never come up in his records for anything."

"Okay, I will admit that it isn't much, but the fact remains that something happened to them, and chances are it was here in town, so I have to think the sheriff will look into any and all possibilities that are presented to him."

"Yeah."

"Especially if Deputy Taylor thought it was enough to check it out himself."

He nodded.

"And then disappeared on top of it," she added.

"I know. I just hate waiting and wish I could be doing something. It's like, what if she is somewhere on that farm right now suffering, all while the sheriff takes his sweet ass time to go visit since it doesn't seem like a priority to him."

She didn't reply to that.

"What if I could help her?" As soon as he said it, he wished he had kept the thought to himself simply because of how ridiculous it was. To his surprise, she didn't say anything about it being a silly idea. Instead –

"That'd be very romantic."

And that's the problem. He kept seeing himself going in

to rescue her as if it were a movie rather than real life.

In real life most people are killed within forty-eight hours of disappearing, he told himself. Though startling, the thought was not as upsetting as it should have been, mostly because he knew it would bring closure. Not just on the 'what happened' question, but on the potential for their future together. Her death, while horrible and heartbreaking, would put an end to the constant thoughts on whether or not they would ever be a couple again.

Sophia opened her Mountain Dew and took a sip. A grimace followed.

"What's wrong?" he asked.

"Nothing, I just forgot how sweet this stuff is." She took another sip. "Ugh, I can't drink it."

"Do you want something else?" He fished in his pocket for more quarters. "I'll take that if you don't want it."

"It was all they had. Everything else was sold out."

"Oh." He wondered if he had gotten the last of the Root Beer then. That and the Mountain Dew had been all that was left last night, and knowing he needed sleep, the latter was the last thing he had wanted.

"But thanks anyway."

He nodded.

Silence settled.

Then, "We could also go get something better. It's not like we have to sit here and wait for the sheriff to call."

"Okay."

"And if you're hungry or anything, I'll get us something for lunch," he added. "Though it's my guess you don't want to go to the diner and that's the only place I know about around here."

"Oh, um, there really isn't any other places in town. We'd have to go over by I-80 or maybe hop onto I-39 and follow it to an exit that has food places."

"Is there anything down by the sheriff station?" He liked the idea of getting out and doing something as a way of keeping his mind occupied, but not driving very far to do it.

"Actually, yeah, there are a couple places. My aunt would kill me for recommending them since they are the closest competition, but –

Scott's phone buzzed.

"Chief Delevan," he said to Sophia while looking at the screen. Then, into the phone, "Hello?"

Nothing.

"Hello, Chief, is that you?"

No words followed, but the connection was there and then, without warning, he heard several loud pops followed by the cry of "fucker" from a female.

Was that Holly?

A part of his mind was confident that it had been, but another thought he was just hoping it to be her. Either way, something was going on wherever the chief was – or at least wherever his phone was – something that was resulting in several screams from both a man and woman.

"What is it?" Sophia asked, concern present.

Scott didn't answer right away, ear trying to pick up something that would give a solid answer on what was happening, but then things went quiet. The call, however, was not disconnected. "I don't know what's going on," he said. "It's the chief's phone and everything, but all I'm getting it background stuff. He's not saying anything."

"You mean like a butt call?" Sophia suggested.

"Exactly like a butt call," Scott said, memories of other such calls, usually while people were driving, flowing through his mind. "And I think . . ." hesitation gripped him for a moment ". . . I think I heard Holly."

"What, are you sure?"

"Yes . . . no . . . I don't know, I think so but . . ." he shook his head and left it at that.

"What was she saying?" Sophia asked.

"I just heard her screaming 'fucker' at someone after gunshots I think."

"Gunshots?"

"I think so."

"And what makes you think it was her screaming?"

"She used to scream at drivers on the road when she was driving and it sounded the same." Picturing one of those moments, he could easily fit the voice he had just heard into the angry screams she always let loose.

He put the phone back to his ear to listen some more, but nothing else was said.

Jonathan

His ankle twisted the wrong way upon landing, causing a small cry to escape his lips as he fell to the ground. Waiting for the pain to fade was not an option, however, so he quickly forced himself back to his feet and hurried toward the door. Two bullets and a scream were directed his way during this dash, the girl able to reach a point on the loft that allowed for a partial view of the doorway. Thankfully, neither shot was true to the mark and he made it through the door without incident.

How many was that? he pondered once he was out upon the gravel, body spread like a snow angle, lungs heaving in and out. *Five? Six?*

She had shot at him twice while he had been up on the loft ledge before jumping, once as he landed, and then twice more as he fled.

Plus the one you fired.

Horror at what had resulted from that shot filled his head. Adding to it was the realization of how close he had come to being killed, all due to a momentary distraction.

And she knew exactly what she was doing and how you would react.

Thinking this shook him to the core, both because he had not expected such a cunning distraction and because it made him realize he would never win her over. And even if at some point she gave in to him, he would always have the fear that it was a trick, thus, he wouldn't be able to trust her.

Of everything that had occurred, this simple realization was the most upsetting of all. In fact, it was heartbreaking. The first girl he had ever really had a chance to start a family with, and she was rejecting him. Even worse, he understood why she was, her mind being stuck on being his captive. Why she couldn't grasp the idea that she could come live with him in the house in complete harmony was beyond him, but she didn't.

And she will do whatever it takes to kill you.

Even if it means being stuck up there without food and water until she dies.

Thinking about this was a huge blow as well. She would rather *die* then be with him. Anyone that wasn't saddened by such a realization wasn't human.

Make it a reality.

Huh?

If she doesn't want to be with you, what's the point of keeping her? Running the farm is hard enough without having to care for captives.

Especially with a scarecrow threatening the house once again, his mind added.

But I can't just kill her.

Or can I?

At this point, it could be considered self-defense given that she had just tried to kill him.

Unless it's possible to disarm her.

If he could do this then the idea of self-defense was nullified.

Does she even have any more bullets in the gun?

He counted the shots again. Six had been fired.

Now the question was how many had been in there to start with. Eight. Ten. Twelve -- if they even went that high. He hadn't looked at the clips, nor had he counted how many rounds he had fired earlier with the first one, his mind mostly focused on figuring out how to change the clip once it had been emptied. Knowing how many rounds were in the clip just hadn't seemed important at the time. Heck, he didn't even know if it was possible to see how many were in it once the clip was loaded, though it would be easy to check. He still had a clip from the deputy in his kitchen.

The sight of the deputy's mutilated face entered his mind once more and would not leave; disgust at what he had been forced to do filling him.

Is he dead?

It was hard to imagine someone surviving such a wound, yet when he had walked over to the crumpled body he had noticed the chest rising and falling with breath.

If not now, he will be soon.

Given the amount of blood that had squirted out, blood that was still on him, he couldn't see him lasting another hour. Unless the blood had just been an initial thing that had stopped shortly after the first few spurts, which would mean he could now be laying up there in agony.

Without a jaw, he wouldn't be able to eat, and whatever medical attention was needed for such a wound was beyond his capabilities.

He's going to die.

And you didn't even get the uniform.

His hope had been that he could wear the uniform and drive the squad car to the motel to confront the young man, the idea that he was a deputy investigating things leading the boy into a false sense of security. What exactly he would do from that point hadn't been realized yet, though he had planned on leaving the squad car there so it wouldn't be linked to the farm and taking the guy's car back. Now, however, that entire plan was scrapped. Even if he could get to the deputy without fear of being shot, the uniform would be bloodstained and unusable.

Could still drive the car out there though.

You need to get rid of it no matter what should other deputies arrive.

He wasn't certain more would come, but given all that had happened, knew it was a strong possibility. He also knew they would want to look around.

Ridding yourself of the deputy's car won't be enough, not unless you find a better place for the girl.

He thought about the root cellar, body shivering.

Would they look in there?

If they came and searched the barn chances were they would search the house as well.

And ask questions about your parents.

They will take you away.

All because those two showed up to take pictures.

All because –

He stopped, an odd vibration against his butt startling him. He then realized it was the phone he had taken from the chief.

Just a number was present on the screen, no name.

Hesitation gripped him.

Would a lack of an answer be an issue?

What if it was the young man from the car asking if everything was okay?

Unsure if it was the right move, he touched the icon on the screen to answer the call and said, "Yes?"

"Chief Delevan, is that you?" The voice belonged to a young man, probably the one from the car earlier, though he couldn't tell for certain.

"Um . . . no," Jonathan said, voice trying to sound puzzled. "Sorry."

"No problem," the voice said.

The call ended.

Jonathan stared at the phone, his hand expecting to feel the vibration once again as the young man attempted to call the correct phone.

No vibration arrived.

After that, he stared at the screen for several seconds trying to figure out how the phone actually worked so he could check the call log. What he found once he had uncovered the process startled him. Not too long ago he had placed a call to the number that had just called. How exactly he had done that he didn't know, but he had.

Also noted was that the young man had called the phone a few hours earlier, which meant he had to know that he had the correct number and would have called it again if he felt he had made a mistake the first time around.

But he didn't.

What does that mean?

Concern began to build.

Too much had occurred in the last two days for him to feel comfortable with how things were playing out. He needed to rid himself of everything that connected him with all the people who were on the farm, and his parents' car.

And how are you going to do that?

Just walking into the barn now could result in him being shot.

Find out how many bullets the last clip has.

Once that knowledge was obtained, he would have a pretty good idea of how many rounds she still had and what his possible options were.

* * *

The clip held ten rounds, which meant, unless he had missed a shot, that she had four rounds left. He didn't like that. Just stepping into the barn could prove disastrous, especially if she was standing on the loft-waiting, gun aimed at the doorway.

She has to stand to be able to target the doorway.

How long could she manage that?

He had a feeling her body wouldn't be able to tolerate being on its feet for hours, and if he moved quickly, he could get beneath the loft before she would have a chance to stand up and take aim. And with any luck, she would fire a few rounds toward the door as she did it, wasting her advantage.

Still risky.

Frustration arrived, especially since he felt like he was on a time crunch. Fear of people like the sheriff, his deputies, or some other law enforcement agency that he didn't even know about arriving made it so he couldn't simply wait her out. Had she obtained the gun two weeks ago he simply would have stopped feeding her. Now such a tactic would take too long.

Scott

A call to the sheriff about what he had heard on the phone followed by it being picked up by a person who wasn't Chief Delevan wasn't met with enthusiasm. In fact, though they didn't come right out and say it, he felt as if the words 'please stop calling us with this type of thing' had been passed on to him through the tone of voice used to reassure him that they were doing everything possible.

"If they were doing everything possible they would be at that house right now!" Scott said once the call was ended. "Fuck!"

Sophia didn't reply.

He shook his head. "I just don't get it. Every time I talk to the police they don't want to listen to me."

"Deputy Taylor listened to you, and so did the chief," Sophia said.

Scott sighed. "Yeah, I know, you're right." He looked out the window for a moment, eyes drifting over the sea of corn that seemed to extend beyond the horizon. "I'm sorry, I'm just frustrated."

"No need to apologize. I would be too."

"I really just want to go there now and figure out what is going on, you know. It seems so obvious to me that something is fucked up and all it would take is one visit to find out for sure."

"But that one visit could result in something horrible happening to you."

"But see, I really don't think it will. I'm not sure why,

but for some reason I have this feeling that going there is what I need to do." *And by not going, I'm messing with the way things are supposed to play out.* He kept this second part to himself given how ridiculous it would probably sound.

"Hmm, it's possible."

He didn't say anything after that, not when it was obvious to him that she didn't share his thoughts on this.

Not long after that, he began to wish he had his own car here, his determination to find out once and for all what had happened to Holly guiding him toward the house. Unfortunately, it was still sitting in the chief's driveway.

Better yet, you should have just gone into the fields with the chief. Doing this would have allowed them to watch each other's back, which could have prevented whatever had occurred from actually occurring.

Questions on how and what had happened to the chief followed this thought. It seemed that if he had stayed concealed in the fields as planned then nothing unwanted should have occurred, not unless the family had been out there for some reason and stumbled upon him.

Or maybe he saw something he had to act upon and got fucked while doing it?

But why not call and tell me?

One simple phone call and things could have been different. One simple phone call and the sheriff may have taken things more seriously given the information they had obtained.

He looked at his phone and considered calling the chief again to see if he could get any information from the person who had answered.

Just accuse them of harming the chief and see what happens. Or ask him where Holly is.

A few seconds later he put the phone away, fear of making the family panic, which could lead them to doing something horrible to Holly – if she was even still alive – guiding his hand.

Frustration followed.

He felt so useless.

He needed to do something.

"I'm sorry," Sophia said. "I know this is really hard."

"Yeah."

"And I wish I could offer some better advice than waiting to see what the sheriff says."

"It's okay. I can't think of anything else either. That's what really sucks. I want to be doing something, but there isn't anything I really can do."

"I know what you mean."

The two went silent after that and stayed that way for nearly ten minutes, Scott pacing the small room while Sophia sat on the bed watching, a hand toying with a necklace she had pulled from within her sweatshirt.

* * *

"I don't know," Sophia said. "I could get in trouble."

"No you won't," Scott said. "Trust me."

"But they might think it's a prank." She shook her head. "It's too risky. Plus, after all the calls you've made they know about the farm and the possibility that something is going on. There isn't anything more we can do on that end."

He sighed. "Yes, I've made a lot of calls, but they don't seem to be doing anything about it. That's why a call from another person, someone completely unconnected to all this, would help. They can't ignore it after that."

"Scott, you need to calm down and give them time. They will look into it. You just have to give them a chance."

"My girlfriend's life could be at stake here!" he shouted. She jumped.

He held up a hand and apologized.

She didn't reply.

"If you don't want to call that's fine, just do me a favor," he said.

"What?"

"Can you drive me to my car? It's at the chief's place."

"Um . . . okay." Despite the words, she didn't stand up from the bed.

He waited.

"What're you going to do?" she asked.

"I don't know." It wasn't a complete lie. In his mind he saw himself going to the farm, he just didn't know at what point he would do it. "Maybe nothing if the sheriff calls while we are driving."

"Please don't go to the farm."

"I have no choice."

"Yes you do," she urged. "Everything is a choice."

She was right, everything was a choice. Even so, he knew what decision he had to make, thus, despite being presented with options, he could only choose one answer. Saying this, however, would be pointless. She wasn't going to agree with him no matter what. And he understood why. If he were in her shoes, he would be arguing against it as well.

"Just wait for the sheriff to do something. A deputy is missing. He will act. Probably is as we speak."

"Then why doesn't he tell me that?" Scott demanded.

"Because he's probably being stubborn. You've pummeled him with calls and he doesn't want to make you feel like you influenced him. It's all his decision. He's in charge and he decides what to do. But he also knows he has to do something. Leaving this situation uninvestigated would be a risk to his career."

Several minutes passed, Scott having resumed his

stance at the window, eyes focused on some farm
structure way off in the distance. From there he shifted his
focus to Sophia's reflection, her fingers now toying with
an earring.

She is worried.

*Two days ago, she had no idea you even existed, yet now she
is worried about you.*

He didn't know what to make of that and eventually let
the thought fade.

His phone vibrated.

Thinking it was the sheriff he quickly pulled it from his
pocket and looked at the screen. Frustration followed. It
was his mother.

"Who was it?" Sophia asked as he hit IGNORE.

"My mom. We talk every Sunday. I totally forgot it
was that time."

"Does she know what you're doing?"

"No. She'd think it was ridiculous and tell me I need to
move on." *Something she thinks I've already done,* he silently
added. Talks with her on how he felt about the Holly
situation had never gone well simply because she always
tried to make him realize there was nothing he could do.
Holly made a decision and that was it. He couldn't
change her mind.

'I have to try, though,' he always replied. 'I won't be
able to live with myself if I don't.'

And now he had the same feelings. If he didn't do
something, if he didn't go to the farm and then later found
out something had happened to her this evening, he
would not be able to live with himself. His love for her
was too strong. The events of the past didn't matter.
Anything he could do for her he would do, even if she
never reciprocated.

If I go there, find them, and save them and they decide to stay together, I will be okay with it.

Or will I?

Could she actually stay with Ethan after something like this, all while ignoring what he had done?

He didn't think such a thing was possible.

Sadly, this thought brought about concern over his own motivation, which was why he was glad he hadn't shared it with Sophia. Sure, he hoped they would get back together once all this was said and done, but if they didn't, at least he could live with the satisfaction of knowing he had saved her life.

And she will always know it too.

He looked at Sophia's reflection again and saw her stretch backward on the bed, chest thrust out to pop her back. The display was erotic, and caught him off guard.

Would I give in if she tried to use her body to keep me from going to the farm? he wondered, the thought coming out of nowhere.

The question was probably pointless because he doubted she would go such a route.

We shall see.

He turned.

She straightened and looked at him, waiting.

"Let's go get my car."

Holly

Firing the pistol was different than she expected it would be, the kick less forceful than she had anticipated, yet still powerful enough to create a tingle within her arm. It also was harder to hit things, her first shot having completely missed Jonathan despite how close he had been. In fact, had he simply held still, he probably could have caused her to expend all the bullets as she tried to hit him, each shot implanting itself somewhere else in the barn despite her sense that the barrel was locked in on his body.

Then again, if she had hit him, he probably would have fallen from the loft given how close to the edge he had been, thus ending her chances of being able to retrieve the padlock key.

If he even had it on him.

The thought of shooting him dead and then learning she still had no chance at freedom made her legs go weak and she had no choice but to sit down, chain clinking as part of the slack coiled.

She then wondered how long she could have survived in such a situation, and how horrible those final days would be given that she had two rotting bodies sharing the space.

Three days without water, she reminded herself, but then wondered if she could push it longer by drinking other fluids. Maybe five or six days?

What about blood?

Would it be okay to drink or would the lack of life within the bodies cause it to become useless?

Can you even really drink blood?

Doesn't it make you sick?

At some point, somewhere, she had heard this, possibly during a class or maybe from a TV show. Not that it really mattered. She didn't have two bodies up here, her skill with a firearm so awful that using the word pathetic was probably too good for what she had displayed.

You might still have to resort to such drastic measures, though, she told herself, her mind suddenly wondering if Jonathan would continue to care for her after this. Would he even be willing to enter the barn knowing he could be shot? She wouldn't. And without him . . .

She didn't want to continue this line of thought, though, truthfully, she couldn't really stop her mind from playing it out, an image of her growing sick from trying to eat the deputy's body as hunger got the best of her filling her head.

Is he dead yet?

A few minutes earlier, she had been able to hear a gentle wheeze coming from his mouth area, but now that had faded. His chest had also gone still.

Though she wanted to be sad, no emotion would arrive. It just wasn't there. Seeing his body didn't bring forth anything but a sense of discomfort and amazement at how quickly things could be fucked up.

But at least we tried.

The inner statement was an attempt at rationalizing and bringing honor to what had happened. He hadn't just sat by and waited to be killed. He had tried to escape, and almost succeeded.

Yeah, but he's still dead.

The finality of that pretty much ended her attempts at

adding anything to what had occurred.

She shook her head.

* * *

How many bullets are left?

The thought came out of nowhere as she sat in the loft, body once again aching from the trauma it had endured now that the adrenaline from the final moments had worn off.

Is it even possible to tell?

She turned the gun over several times, hands careful not to point it at herself or to jar the trigger, eyes wondering if there was any indicator mark that could help answer the question. Memories of squirt gun fights as a kid arrived for some reason while thinking this, her eyes always able to see the level of water in the thin plastic tank that attached to the gun.

Nothing on the pistol helped her with the question and since she had no idea how to pull the bullet clip free, nor did she want to figure it out for fear that she might not be able to get it back in, she decided she would just have to live with the mystery.

Not that it really mattered. Wasn't like she could hit anything. Not unless she had the gun pressed against the object and pulled the trigger.

Doubt he will get that close.

I'd probably have a better chance of throwing the pistol at him. Her aim with a softball during high school had always been true, so nailing him in the head probably wouldn't be too difficult.

Though with my luck the gun would hit the loft, fire, and hit me.

She shook her head at the thought, and then wondered what Jonathan's next move would be.

Probably try to sneak in here once I'm asleep and take the gun.

The thought was chilling because it would probably be successful. Already her exhaustion was threatening to overtake her, her body craving the dirty straw pile she had called a bed for the last two weeks.

Maybe sleep now so that I'm awake later when he thinks I'll be asleep.

Wait for him to get close, put the gun to his stomach and pull the trigger.

Would it work?

Even if it does, what if he doesn't have the key? What am I going to do then, shoot the chain?

The thought, which wasn't supposed to be a serious one at all, brought everything to a halt.

Was such a thing possible?

Were the bullets in the gun powerful enough to sever one of the links?

She lifted the chain while contemplating this, her hand trying to conclude something, anything, by the weight. Nothing useful arrived, however.

What about the lock?

Shooting that seemed a better option given that it would be harder for the bullet to be deflected, and would probably do quite a bit of damage to the mechanisms within.

Will it do enough?

What if it twists them around so much that it becomes impossible to free the link holding the chains together?

This question once again brought to mind how many bullets were in the gun. If it held more than one or two then chances were good she could shoot the lock enough times to free herself. If it was just one, she might do nothing more than create a jagged hunk of metal that constantly tore at her every time she shifted positions.

The proximity of the padlock to her body was a bit frightening as well. She had no idea what kind of bullets were in the gun or how they would react when coming in contact with the metal object, but did know ricochet was a possibility thanks to an episode of *Mythbusters* she had once watched with Scott.

You have to try.

Determination arrived, but rather than just press the gun barrel to the lock and fire she decided to contemplate it for a while so she could figure out the best position to be in for the act. At the same time, she knew there really wasn't more than one position she could be in while carrying it out, the chain and lock tight against her body, which meant she had to sit in a way that allowed the lock to rest on the loft surface and then press the barrel against it. The question was could she do anything to protect her body? Was there anything up here to act as a buffer?

Nothing jumped out at her.

She was just going to have to do it as she was and hope for the best.

She took a deep breath and then twisted herself into position, left hand bracing herself while the right pressed the barrel up against the surface of the padlock.

Another deep breath.

Now or never.

She pulled the trigger.

Jonathan

The gunshot reached his ears as he was getting some water, a trip down into the root cellar where he thought he could put the girl once he had her disarmed – if he didn't have to kill her – having left his mouth feeling dusty. Anxiety had nearly overcome him as well, memories of being locked down there with the snakes too much to bear. Thoughts on how the punishment hadn't been fair entered his mind; thoughts that he had feared were sinful as a child but now wondered about such claims. His father, having been bitten by a rat while working in the root cellar before dawn one day, had instructed him to get some snakes from the field and put them down there. Wanting to be a good son, Jonathan had suppressed his fear of the serpents while also closing his ears to any attempts by them to make him question God, and carried them down one bucket full at a time. All day he did this, his mind determined to make his father proud. Instead, his father had come in from working in the far fields at dinnertime and, once he realized how many snakes were now down there, was furious with him.

'One or two was all we needed!' he had screamed.

'I didn't know!' Jonathan had echoed back, lips quivering, tears falling.

A backhanded blow had followed, his father claiming he had talked back. His mother had then joined in, statements on how he had purposely defied them arising.

'But it isn't your fault,' she added. *'Satan spoke through the serpents to encourage such an act.'*

'No, I made sure he didn't and closed my ears,' Saying this was a mistake, their opinion being that he had then either defied them on purpose thinking it would be funny to have all these snakes in the cellar, or Satan had really spoken to him and he was protecting him. Whichever it was, he needed to be taught a lesson. Five days later, they released him from the root cellar, body weak from all the watery bowels he had experienced from some jarred goods he had eaten, and covered in snakebites. It had been a horrifying experience, especially at night when he couldn't see anything in the darkness. Making it worse was that the snakes would try to warm themselves by curling up with his body while he slept, which in turn would cause him to panic upon waking. Nasty bites would follow.

Just thinking about those days and nights made him shiver. It had been one of the worst experiences of his life, one that he never wanted to endure again. He also didn't want anyone else to go through it, which was why he had put the boy and girl in the barn two weeks earlier. It had been the only place besides the root cellar that he could think of. Now, however, he knew he would have to change it. The barn wasn't secure enough, not if more deputies came. Thankfully, having carefully searched the root cellar, it seemed the snakes were now long gone. He also hadn't spotted any rats. Even so, he didn't like the idea of putting the girl down there, or having to go down there on a daily basis to feed her.

You have no choice.

If you get the gun away from her, you will have to do something, and can't leave her in there.

Even without the threat of police intervention, the barn was no place for a person during the winter months. She would freeze to death.

You should never have put them there to begin with.

You should have just let them leave.

Even as he thought this, concerns about them telling people about the car arrived, justifying his actions. He had had no choice. One couldn't control the events that unfolded; they could just react to them, which is what he had done.

A second gunshot echoed as he went to the door, dry mouth forgotten, hands grabbing the shotgun.

A quick check of the barrel showed the fresh shells within, something he knew would be the case having loaded it earlier, but still had to verify.

A third gunshot.

What is she shooting at?

Scarecrow?

Thinking this, he hurried upstairs to the window to check the field, eyes horrified at what they might see – well, might not see, actually.

The scarecrow was still on its perch, which meant she was shooting at something else.

She has one round left, he realized while heading back downstairs to the front door.

One more shot and he wouldn't have to worry about disarming her, not unless he miscounted how many times the gun had been fired.

Maybe just kill her anyway.

No, you'll want her around once the End Times come.

Are they really going to come?

They have already started.

Once civilization collapsed and she recognized how horrible things were, she would realize why he had done what he had done and connect with him. It had to happen. How anyone could still resist in such a time was beyond him. She would be his wife once the gates of Hell were opened and the legions of the damned released upon the world.

The question was could he wait that long? Could he put up with her continued resistance until then?

Hopefully the answer was yes.

Try to remember you need her. Once things get bad, her companionship and the God-fearing children the two of you will produce will be invaluable. She will take on the role your parents always wanted for Naomi, though without the full purity of the family bloodline.

Shotgun ready, yet hoping he wouldn't have to use it on her, Jonathan stepped out of the house and started toward the barn.

Fire one more time, he pleaded. *Just one more time!*

The sound of gravel crunching beneath tires reached his ears.

He turned.

Dust was rising up on the driveway, though whatever vehicle that was producing it was still unseen.

Horrified, both by the gunshots and coming intruder, Jonathan ducked into the nearest patch of corn and waited. Not long after that, a sheriff deputy squad car pulled up, the deputy within glancing all around as he maneuvered the car into the center of the gravel circle.

Heart racing, and a curse threatening to leave his lips, Jonathan waited, mind and body unsure what to do.

The deputy stepped out of the car; his movements slow as he continued to scan everything.

Jonathan thought about charging forward and shooting him, but knew his skills with the shotgun were not up to the task and that chances were the deputy would shoot him first.

Unless God is on your side.

God is probably the reason you're hesitating.

But why am I thinking of doing it at all then?

Free will.

He shook the thoughts away and focused on the deputy. The silence of the farm was almost too much to bear, especially after the gunshots.

Thoughts on what had occurred within the barn entered his mind, but went nowhere. He wouldn't know anything until he actually was able to see inside himself, or forced Holly to tell him.

What if the deputy turned into a scarecrow and attacked her? Could that happen?

Did one have to be placed upon the post to be a scarecrow, or could it happen with anyone if the evil forces at work wished it?

No answer arrived.

The new deputy started toward the house, but then stopped and twisted around as the barn door opened, its hinges squealing.

"Help me," Holly cried while stumbling out, right hand holding the gun and the left her lower abdomen. Blood stood out upon that hand. It wasn't much, yet was enough for him to see it even with the distance between them.

Startled, the deputy twisted around, his gun drawn.

"Please!" Holly added.

"Drop the gun," the deputy ordered.

Holly didn't right away, her feet taking her a few more steps toward him.

"Drop the gun!"

This time she complied, and then, as if the gun had been part of her strength, fell down next to it.

A debate on what to do continued within Jonathan.

His back is too me.
You could charge him.
Do it!

Moving carefully so as to not make a sound, Jonathan emerged from the corn, shotgun leveled upon the deputy's back.

Scott

"I really don't think you should be doing this," Sophia said. The two were standing in the chief's driveway, a knock on the door followed by a peek through the garage window solidifying the theory that he had never returned from the Turner farm.

Which means the young man from the truck probably moved the car, Scott said to himself, his mind certain that the boy had belonged to the Turner family. To Sophia, he said, "I have to."

"But why?" she asked.

"What if she's alive right now, but then killed later tonight? How could I live with myself knowing that I could have prevented that?"

Sophia just stared at him.

"I couldn't," he added. "It would haunt me forever."

"But you've done so much already, all for a girl that doesn't even want you."

Scott didn't know how to reply to that. He also felt stung even though she spoke the truth. Actually, it being the truth was probably the reason it stung.

"Why not give the sheriff just a little more time. I'm sure he's going to send someone. He has to."

"I can't," he said and started toward his car, keys in hand. "I know it's hard to understand and seems crazy, but . . . well, I have to do this."

She didn't reply.

He got into his car and started the ignition.

Sophia came up and knocked on the window.

"Yeah?" he asked while rolling it down.

"Just . . . be careful, okay? We both know something is wrong there, so don't be careless and . . . don't try to be . . ." she shook her head ". . . if she is still alive it's probably because they're keeping her alive for a reason, so don't race in as if they are going to kill her a few minutes later."

Scott didn't know what to say and simply nodded.

"And keep me posted on what is going on."

"I will." He hesitated, still unsure what to say. "Please try not to worry," he finally said. "I'm not going to let anything happen. I think the others didn't fully understood what they were walking into. They thought their status as law enforcement people would keep them safe. I won't make that mistake."

She didn't reply, probably because she didn't agree with his line of thought. Truth was, he didn't fully believe it himself, but wasn't going to admit that, not when she was obviously worried about his well-being.

Two days ago, she didn't even know who I was, and now . . . he wasn't sure what to make of this, and let the thought fade away. Later, he could think upon it, and what it possibly meant, in more detail, but right now, he needed to focus.

* * *

Wish I had a gun, he said to himself a few minutes later while driving, memories of the shotgun on the seat of the truck filling his head. Then again, Deputy Taylor had had one and had still disappeared. *And he was probably trained in how to use it.* The only 'training' Scott had ever had came from video games and one paintball experience, and he hadn't been able to hit anyone during that.

Still, just the threat of a gun could be an advantage; one he wished he were in possession of.

But you aren't, and there is no way to change it.
Unless the chief had one.
Should have checked his house.

Thinking about this led him to wonder why the chief wouldn't have brought a gun himself. Chances were, given his former career, he had at least one, yet at no point had he ever made its presence known despite being certain the Turner family was dangerous.

Then again, maybe he did have one, but didn't say anything. If so, that really didn't bode well for him. Two members of law enforcement, both armed, disappearing while searching the farm.

Maybe you really should just wait and see what happens with the sheriff.

No.

He had to do this. As reckless as it was, he had no choice. He --

Sophia's car appeared behind him, its turn onto the road occurring just seconds before he turned off, almost as if she were trying to keep a distance so he wouldn't notice her following him.

But why would she be following me?

First, she knew where he was going, so following wouldn't be needed; second, she could have come with if she wanted.

She's probably just going home and this is the route she needs to take.

A turn northward loomed ahead. He made it and then watched the rearview mirror to see if she would make it as well, his speed slowing a bit so he wouldn't lose sight of the intersection.

Ten seconds turned into twenty seconds and then into thirty. At the fifty-second mark, her car finally made an appearance as it crossed the intersection.

She wasn't following him.

He sighed and then chided himself for even considering such a possibility. There simply was no purpose for such an act. It was silly.

* * *

It took a while for him to find the farm, the fact that he hadn't been driving during either of the two visits making it so his body didn't fully remember the exact route that needed to be taken. Once in the general area, however, it was just a matter of time until he recognized something; the grid pattern layout of the roads helping quite a bit since each grid seemed to enclose a farm.

And then of course there was the knowledge that the Turner farm was the end of the line for a while, the local river boarding much of it along with tangled up scrubland. 'They kind of got the worst of worst when it came to the land,' Chief Delevan had said while driving. 'Their first farmer generation taking what no one else wanted.'

A question on *why* had followed, but the chief had no real answer, just speculation, much of which seemed derived from his thoughts on the present generation. Because of this, Scott didn't put too much stock in it, his thinking being the original farming generation hadn't been trying to isolate themselves, but instead hadn't really known any better. It also seemed like they had done okay with the land, the corn crop looking as if it usually provided a pretty good yield, this year being an exception due to the drought. That was hurting everyone though, not just them.

But it could have been viewed differently by them, especially if their focus on religion was as warped as the chief had claimed, he told himself, his mind trying to match this up with a reason on why the disappearances had occurred. Nothing would really connect, however, and truth was, if they were crazy, then the reason probably wouldn't make much sense to anyone but them.

If she is still alive it's because they are keeping her alive for something, Sophia had said.

Though it seemed ridiculous, he wondered if they could be planning or had already carried out some bizarre Old Testament style of sacrifice to try to end the drought. It seemed crazy, but then again, many of the things carried out in the name of religion were, thus, the possibility existed.

With this thought, he stepped out of the car and headed into the corn, his route nearly identical to the one Chief Delevan had taken earlier. Whether or not this was a wise decision he didn't know, but deep down inside he had a feeling it didn't really matter. What did was whatever actions he took once he was at the farm, actions that needed to be well thought out.

Holly

Holding the gun against the lock was a mistake, the kickback as the bullet met the hardened metal throwing her arm up and away at a painful angle and causing her to toss the pistol. The explosion also hurt her ear in a way that it hadn't when firing at Jonathan, a PING-like vibration hitting hard and causing her to wince.

It's gotta be the way you were leaning over the gun, she told herself while regaining her composure, her gun hand rubbing at her ear while her left hand rubbed at the sore forearm.

A second later, she checked the padlock.

Though damaged, it was still secure.

Where's the gun?

It didn't take long to find the pistol, the involuntary toss having had very little force behind it. At the same time, she was lucky it hadn't gone any further, the slack in the chain just enough for her to reach it where it was. Another couple of feet and she would have really had to stretch herself to grab it – if such a stretch were even possible.

Fortunately it wasn't out of reach and soon she was in position again, body ready to shoot the lock again, muzzle held an inch away this time in hopes that her arm wouldn't be kicked back.

No kickback occurred, though the loud PING! hit her

eardrum once again and caused her to cry out in pain. A burning sensation in her calf followed, a hot piece of metal having landed upon her pant leg and burned through.

The lock still held, but given the damage, she was sure one more bullet would do the trick.

Hope there is one more bullet.

With her luck, the gun would be empty.

One more time.

She touched the muzzle to the area she wanted to put the bullet and then raised it a bit.

Hesitation arrived.

She took a deep breath and pulled the trigger.

A blast echoed followed by a horrible ripping sensation in her abdomen.

Startled by the pain, she dropped the gun and grabbed her side. Blood met her fingers.

She twisted around so she could better see the damage, panic starting to rise.

Had the bullet bounced off and ripped through her?

Was she going to die.

Blood oozed, her panic increasing.

And the pain was intense.

Fuck!

You gotta get help.

Free yourself, get off the farm, and get to a hospital.

Where's the gun?

She found it lying by her side, a small amount of smoke still leaving the muzzle. Sitting next to it was the padlock, the distorted hunk of metal looking nothing like the locking mechanism she had needed to free herself from.

One more shot, her mind decided while slowly lifting the gun and positioning it against the padlock.

A heavy *thunk* as the chain fell from her body echoed but didn't fully register. In fact, it wasn't until she pushed at the padlock with the muzzle to better position things when she realized the chain was no longer linked through it.

Fuck, it worked.

You're free.

A new type of panic set in, one that made her fear the sudden appearance of Jonathan given that she actually had a chance at getting away. Making it worse was that she knew he had to have heard the gunshots and was probably going to be making an appearance soon.

Unless he is worried about being shot himself, she said while standing, the pain in her side growing more intense as everything shifted.

An image of him waiting just outside the barn door, shotgun ready, entered her head. If there, he would have a serious advantage over her, the shotgun probably able to hit everything within the open doorway while she had to actually have skill with her firearm to hit him.

But maybe he isn't there.

Maybe he hasn't even heard the –

The sound of a car pulling up reached her ears.

Someone was outside.

The police?

Scott?

Some unexpected local person just coming by to chitchat?

This final idea seemed the most absurd. Jonathan wouldn't have visitors like that. Still, someone was out there and whoever it was could possibly help her. First things first, however, she had to get to them.

And warn them!

Deputy Taylor had been surprised by the boy. She didn't want the same thing to happen again.

Getting onto the ladder was awkward with the gun and painful, yet her determination to get down and escape helped her overcome this and soon she was moving toward the barn door, gun ready to fire if needed, lips ready to shout a warning.

A plea for help was what left her, the sight of the deputy and his car – one that he could easily drive her away in within seconds – nearly overwhelming her.

Not long after that, she was on the ground, her body having given out for some reason despite her need to get into the car. She was just too exhausted and in too much pain.

"Help me," she said as the deputy came close, his gun no longer leveled upon her but still ready to be used should the need arise.

She then spotted Jonathan coming out of the corn moving toward them, the shotgun in his hands.

"Don't!" the deputy shouted as she reached for the gun.

"Behind you!" Holly screamed, her lips able to muster up enough force to project the warning despite the overwhelming exhaustion.

The deputy spun.

A blast followed, as did several shots from the deputy, his body falling to the ground as he fired.

"No!" she cried and grabbed the gun, mind certain that he had been hit.

Jonathan wasn't in sight, but that was okay because she knew he was behind the car. Opposite him, also taking cover, was the deputy, his sudden movements to get behind a wheel making her realize he was okay. Or at least okay enough to the point where he could still function.

Was he hit?

Or had he simply fallen as a reflex?

Did he hit Jonathan with any of his rounds?

"Are you okay?" He was looking at her, but she didn't

realize he was asking her a question for several seconds. Once she did, she wasn't sure how to reply, her eyes just wanting to focus on the car so she could see what Jonathan did next.

The deputy shifted, his free hand reaching for his belt. At first, Holly wasn't sure what he was doing, but then realized he had his radio out and was getting ready to make a call.

"This is Andrews at that farm. I need assistance. Repeat, I need – "

Jonathan came around the car, shotgun ready.

The deputy tried to move and bring up his gun, but wasn't fast enough, his head disappearing in a cloud of pink spray as the shotgun fired.

Holly lifted the gun and pulled the trigger.

Jonathan shouted something and fell against the car, shotgun leaving his fingers as he grabbed his upper arm.

"Fuck!" he cried.

Holly kept pulling the trigger, but nothing happened, that bullet having been her last, which she finally realized when she saw the appearance of the gun, the top half open as she had seen in movies whenever a gun was empty.

"FUCK! FUCK! FUCK!" he shouted.

Holly felt satisfaction at the blood she saw, but not at the fact that she had only hit him in the arm. It wasn't enough. She wanted him dead.

Still clutching his arm, Jonathan looked around until he spotted whatever it was that he had been looking for, grabbed it, and then started toward her.

"Please, I'm sorry," she said, and then hated herself for the apology.

The fact that it didn't nullify his anger just made it worse, though given his actions she didn't have time to dwell upon her regret.

Several painful gasps left her lips as he twisted her around so that he could handcuff her hands together. He then started dragging her toward the house by them, her legs kicking against the gravel as she tried to stand.

Jonathan

He took her toward the root cellar, the metal edges of the cuffs and the tiny chain digging into his palm as she fought against every step he took. It was no use, though. She could not stop him. Even with the wound in his arm, she was no match, her attempts at resistance doing nothing but causing her pain -- pain that he wanted to add upon given that all his troubles these past two weeks were because of her. Had she not shown up he simply would have continued running the farm, and while that was stressful in itself, and not going well, it was nothing compared to the problems he now faced.

Two dead deputies, a dead chief of police, a dead boyfriend, and an angry scarecrow that wants nothing more than to eviscerate you.

He groaned at the thought, and then winced as Holly caught the doorway with her foot and tugged back on the handcuffs.

His grip loosened, but did not open completely.

"Let go," he said.

Her foot continued to hold.

Pain laced anger arrived and he used all the strength he could muster to yank her to her feet, a cry leaving her lips as the cuffs dug into her wrists. He then slammed her into the wall, her body attempting to bounce back toward him, but unable to due to his own body pressing into her.

Fear was in her eyes and for some reason it caused a pleasant tingle within him. The realization that his forearm was pressed into her breasts, a nipple actually poking against his skin, added to this and before he knew it, he was rubbing his groin against her.

Disgust appeared upon her face, and her struggles got fiercer, yet were no use. She simply was not strong enough to resist him, even with the wound in his arm, which was even more of a turn on for him. Knowing she was his, knowing that he had power over her --

Pain exploded in his groin, his testicles feeling as if they had been crushed, her knee having shot upward with considerable force.

Legs useless, and lungs seemingly unable to take in air, he started to crumble, yet somehow maintained his grip on her handcuffs.

"Let go!" she demanded while attempting to pull herself free.

His fist stayed tight, his mind determined to hold her until the pain faded and his strength returned.

She was having none of this, however, and tried kicking him while continuing to struggle. The space between them was too small for her to get any momentum though, so her blows were more like little nudges.

No time!

Move!

He tried to stand, his midsection feeling hollow as everything shifted.

She then did something he wasn't expecting. She put her foot against the wall and thrust herself against him, the force enough for him to stumble backward into the table and then trip over a chair, his wounded arm crying out in agony as his body landed upon it, all while she crashed down on top of him thanks to his continued grip on the handcuffs.

"Bitch," he started and then gasped as she kneed him

again, a vomit-like sensation rising within his throat, but not producing anything.

She ripped herself free from his grip, handcuff link catching and tearing his thumbnail.

A burning pain appeared, yet was nothing compared to the agony his testicles were experiencing. It was unlike anything he had ever felt before.

Stop her, his mind demanded as she scrambled to her feet. *Don't let her get –*

The sound of a drawer opening reached his ears.

What is she --

His thought stopped as he heard the unmistakable ring of a blade being pulled free, its surface scraping against the drawer edge.

Pain faded as panic appeared.

He twisted around just as she came at him with the knife, both hands clasped around it due to the handcuffs.

She slashed down at him as he scrambled backward across the floor, her movement awkward given the handcuffs and the obvious pain she was in. Had it not been for this combination, he most certainly would have been cut. He wasn't, however, and managed to get to his knees before the next slash came.

This time her aim was better, the serrated blade ripping open the top of his left hand as he tried to block it, the skin feeling as if it was first snagged by the teeth and then pulled until it split, all while his other hand took hold of her right wrist.

"Drop it," he commanded, voice edged with pain.

She struggled against his grip, but couldn't twist the knife into him. She also couldn't stop her body from moving backward into the counter as he stood up and pressed her with his own.

Pain fought him the entire time, but he didn't let it get

the upper hand, not when his own death would result.

She weakened a bit, his hand feeling the drain as he continued to squeeze her wrist.

"Let go!"

"Go to Hell!"

With that, he lifted her hands up, and then brought them down as hard as he could against the edge of the counter, a crunch reaching his ears before a scream appeared. The knife then clattered against the floor, her broken hand no longer able to grip anything.

Another cry left her lips as he took hold of the broken hand and yanked her toward the fruit cellar door, her feet following his without protest, her mind knowing that any divergence would result in horrific pain as he twisted her hand.

A desire to throw her down the steps was present, but he didn't act upon it. Instead, he rushed her down them, her steps having to be quick so she wouldn't stumble, yet at the same time probably causing her unbearable pain in the wound on her side and hand. Once at the bottom he used the momentum from the stairs to throw her against the wall, her body crashing into it with a heavy *thunk* followed by a gasp as she crumbled to the dirt floor.

Without saying a word, he returned to the kitchen, weary body closing the door and throwing the latch. Later, once he had more time he would bring in a chain and restrain her so she didn't destroy any of the food items they would need for winter. For now he was content to simply let her be, the agony she was in making it unlikely she would attempt anything beyond finding a comfortable position to curl up in.

Actually, he wanted to do the same, his body demanding rest. Taking his body up on it could be disastrous, though.

Did the radio call go through? he wondered.

Does it even matter?

Once the deputy failed to return from this visit, more would come. Of this, he was certain. And once that happened, all would be lost.

So why bother with anything?

Just get in the truck and leave.

Find a new home, one far from here.

The idea had appeal, and honestly, was probably the best option despite the issue of not knowing where to go. At the same time, he didn't want to leave this place. It was his home, and had been in his family for many years, willed to them by God back when the country was still young and expanding.

Would leaving it be an act of disobedience in His eyes or was His hand trying to guide him to a new location, one that was more secure so he could continue His with his plan?

Why did understanding God have to be so difficult?

Why couldn't he just speak to him as he had with the prophets in the Old Testament?

Why --

His thoughts on all this stopped as he looked at the ground where the dead deputy lay, everything about his body appearing as he had left it with the exception of one thing. The gun was gone.

Scott

Jesus Christ! his mind cried as he came upon the body of Chief Delevan, the corpse twisted at a grotesque angle, probably due to the struggling it had made against the wicked looking trap.

It wasn't until he took a few steps closer, feet moving slowly, and his shirt held against his nose due to the smell, when he realized the throat had been cut.

Probably why he didn't call for help, his mind decided. Either that or the pain from the trap had been so intense that he simply couldn't process anything for a while and by the time he could someone had arrived to finish him off.

Why set a trap?

It didn't make any sense, not unless the family had randomly set them up throughout the field.

Or maybe they had trouble with people vandalizing the scarecrow and wanted to teach someone a lesson?

A thought appeared, one that caused him to wince.

What if Holly stepped into a trap?

Could that have been the reason for her disappearing?

Could the family have feared her causing them trouble due to the incident and simply gotten rid of her?

Knees weakening, he had no choice but to lean against the scarecrow.

Something popped.

A retched smell appeared, one far worse than what he had been contending with up until this point. And then he felt something oozing against him as he frantically tried to thrust himself away from the scarecrow.

Maggots!

They were falling from beneath the shirt, his shoulder having pressed into the midsection of the scarecrow.

Gah! One was on his neck. He knocked it away and then rubbed at his back trying to find more. It seemed only one had managed to get on him, thankfully.

He started backing away, but then stopped, mind suddenly wearing of the possibility that more traps were present.

Turning carefully, he started moving away from the scarecrow, eyes watching to make sure he was stepping upon dirt rather than a clump of fallen cornstalk leaves.

After about ten feet, he stopped and took a sip of water, the smell having somehow worked its way into his taste buds. While doing this an idea hit and he pulled out his phone.

* * *

DON'T GO ANY FURTHER, Sophia texted back after receiving the picture of the chief's body. I'M CALLING THE SHERIFF RIGHT NOW!

OKAY, I WON'T, Scott replied. He actually meant it too, a certainty about the sheriff quickly responding to this entering his mind, until he heard the gunshots. Hearing them, and realizing what they were, forced him to act.

Running carefully, his eyes still making sure his foot was landing upon dirt, and arms spread to keep him from being slapped by leaves and actual hunks of rotting corn, he headed toward the farmhouse.

One final blast seemed to echo as he neared, followed by a female scream. It was Holly. Of this, he had no doubt.

Heart racing, he closed the distance between him and the edge of the field, his pace only slowing as he saw the edge looming.

He did send someone, his mind noted upon seeing the deputy's squad car. It sat in the middle of a driveway-like area, right between the farmhouse and barn.

No one was stirring.

Hesitation gripped him. He wasn't sure what to do. Something had just occurred, but what exactly it had been was a mystery. One thing he was sure off, the screams from Holly had come after the gunshots, which meant she had to still be alive. That might not last, however.

Where is everyone?

His phone buzzed.

He checked the message.

THEY SAY SOMEONE SHOULD BE THERE SOON, Sophia said.

TELL THEM I HEARD GUNSHOTS.

Pocketing his phone, he started to work his way around the house and barn while staying in the corn, his hope being to get a better view of things.

Two minutes later, he saw the body on the ground by the deputy's car, and while a part of him knew the guy was dead, another part held some hope that he was just unconscious. This hope faded as he moved toward the car, body crouching low just in case someone looked out from a window, the realization that the oddness of the body was a result of the head being mostly gone.

Seeing this should have sickened him, yet it didn't for some reason, maybe because within a second of seeing the horrific display, his eyes came upon the gun still clutched in the deputy's hand.

A scream from within the house reached his ears.

Grabbing the pistol, the fingers didn't provide the resistance he thought they would (maybe due to freshness?), and the shotgun, he hurried toward the house, but not the front. Instead, he headed toward the back, his eyes attempting to peek into each window as he passed them.

Seeing inside was difficult, however, and after a few attempts he realized it was dangerous given how long he had to press his face against the glass before things within came into focus. Those inside would see him right away.

A back door was present.

Before going in he examined the shotgun, his hands fumbling around with it for several seconds before he figured out how to open it.

Two shells were in the gun, but even with his inexperience, he could tell they had been used, thus the shotgun was useless to him. The pistol, however, seemed good to go, though now he wished he had taken a moment to grab an extra clip from the deputy, if any had been present, questions on just how many rounds had been fired earlier worrying him.

One shot is all you need.

The inner statement did little to build his confidence.

His phone buzzed.

He ignored it and moved toward the backdoor, gun held with two hands and pointed downward.

A window was present in the door, one that he was able to peek through now that the sun wasn't to his back. A kitchen sat beyond the door, empty.

He tested the knob.

It twisted without resistance.

Taking a deep breath, he opened the door and stepped inside.

Blood!

It dotted several areas of the floor and then trailed out into the hallway.

Holly's? he questioned.

Fear at what the answer would be clung to him as he followed the trail.

Jonathan

Panicked, Jonathan scanned the area around him to see if someone was present, his eyes fearing the sudden emergence of a gun-wielding scarecrow. No one was in sight though, and, honestly, he doubted the scarecrow would use a gun. It just didn't seem fitting for some reason, but, as always, he reminded himself of how little he actually knew about such things.

The other gun!

It was sitting on the ground where Holly had dropped it, which was about fifteen feet away. A check of the deputy also provided him with two clips, one of which he quickly loaded into the pistol.

Being in possession of a gun gave him some confidence, but not much given his poor performance with it earlier. He also feared his abilities to confront someone, his body aching from the gunshot, knife wound, and repeated blows to the testicles. Struggling with Holly was one thing, she was weaker than he given her sex, and therefore the injuries didn't really get in the way too much, but if another man was present and armed, things could get ugly.

Where are they?

Having just come from the house, he was pretty sure they weren't there, and decided to move to the barn. It was either that or they were in the corn, which could prove very troublesome.

But why wait in the corn?

If he had been the one waiting with a gun, he would have made a move the second his foe had come out of the house since they would have been completely unaware of the missing gun and a new threat. Because of this, he didn't think whoever was here knew that he knew they were, or that he now had a gun.

But where are they?

Unless they were hiding somewhere within, which didn't make sense given the lack of an attack while his back was turned, he was certain they were not within the barn.

That left the cornfield, which also meant they could now be in the house -- freeing Holly!

So, let them, his mind suggested. *You don't need her for anything. Just get in the truck and leave.*

Though the inner voice had appeal, he couldn't shake the feeling that Holly had been brought to him for a reason and that it was important she be with him during the upcoming events.

Unless she was brought here so events would unfold in such a way as to drive you from this cursed place and start fresh somewhere else?

The question was did the events unfold like this so he would leave by himself or with her? Should he have dragged her to his truck rather than the cellar and simply left?

His eyes settled upon the deputy's car and body while thinking this, a loud answer of YES suddenly appearing in his head. He had made a mistake. As soon as the second deputy had been killed, he should have left the farm. Others would come. The presence of the first deputy should have caused him some serious alarm. In fact, he should have found out who had sent him there and why, and then dealt with that individual. His focus, however, had been on the scarecrow threat, thus he hadn't been able to fully recognize what needed to be done. Now he did, but, sadly, there was a chance that it was too late.

But if God wills it . . .

It seemed that things would work out. If his parents were right and the family had been chosen (him in particular), then no matter what happened God would make sure things unfolded in a way for him to fulfill the plan He had designed for him.

And that plan includes Holly and all the God-fearing children we will bring forth into the new world. He didn't know why, but he was certain of this and therefore felt that leaving her behind would be the equivalent of telling God no – almost as if Moses had dumped a bucket of water on the burning bush and said, 'Sorry dude, your people are screwed.'

Now he had to figure out what to do. Did he wait outside for whoever was around to make an appearance, probably with Holly if that person was inside the house at that moment, or did he go in and confront them, again, if they were inside the house?

It only took a second for him to make the decision, his fear that the sheriff could be sending more deputies this way guiding him toward the house because waiting for them to emerge might take too long – especially if the person who took the gun was waiting for him to make a move.

Front door or back door? he asked himself as he sprinted forward, anxiety spiking.

Front door, he decided, though he wasn't sure why. For all he knew the thought might not even be his own, but that of God guiding him.

No 'might' about it, he is guiding you, so trust the thoughts. Do what must be done. No hesitation. No questions.

Nothing happened during the sprint from the barn to the front door, his fear of attack going unrealized, which meant the person with the gun probably was in the house.

So be it.

He peeked through the window to see if the front entrance was clear. It was.

He opened the door.

Nothing happened.

Moving silently, he stepped inside, gun ready, ears hoping to catch a sound that would alert him to the location of whoever was inside.

All was quiet.

He waited, mind wanting the voice to tell him what to do, but it had gone silent.

Making things worse, the wound in his arm was suddenly throbbing, the run from the barn having created a pulse-like sensation. Sweat had also dripped into it and the open flesh on his hand, adding a nasty sting to both.

Nothing he could do about either, however, so he simply gritted his teeth and continued to listen.

And then it happened.

The floorboards above his head groaned as a step was planted. It wasn't much, yet still enough for him to know it was a person.

And I have the advantage, he told himself.

All he had to do was wait by the stairway, gun ready, and fire upward once the person started their descent. Chances were he would hit them, the narrow area making it almost impossible to miss.

Still, the shotgun would be better.

Sadly, he had no idea where it was. Actually, the person up there might have it for all he knew, though it wouldn't be much use unless he had found the shells in the kitchen. Even then, the advantage of this coming confrontation belonged to him. All he had to do was wait. A few more minutes and the threat this person posed would be eliminated. After that, he would go grab Holly and vacate this place.

But where will we go?

And how will we survive?

No answers arrived, and, after a few seconds, he realized he would just have to put his trust in God and let him guide them. It was all he could do.

Upstairs there was another creak as the floor accepted the weight that was put upon it, the location being his parents' bedroom.

Questions on what the person was doing entered his head, but went without answer. Knowing the why for such a thing was not needed. All that mattered was putting an end to this person so he could leave.

Holly

She wanted nothing more than to pass out, the pain and humiliation of the last several minutes too much to bear. Consciousness remained; however, as did the awful sensation his moist groin had left upon her. That was the worst. Feeling the press of his penis and the excitement leaking from it against her own pubic area had sickened her. Fear had been present as well, fear of what he was going to do the next time they had a quiet moment together.

And you couldn't even stab him!

On the ground, defenseless, body nearly spread as if on a sacrificial altar, and she had done nothing more than cut his hand. It was pathetic. Adding to it was the fact that she had shot him. A bullet had punctured his arm and yet he still was able to overpower her.

You were almost free, again.

Every time he somehow got the upper hand. It didn't seem to matter what was stacked against him, in the end things worked out in his favor, almost as if his statements on God being on his side were true. No one could be this lucky.

But maybe it is coming to an end, the radio call attempt by the deputy having sparked enough concern to bring in backup?

And even if it didn't, it was only a matter of time before someone came to investigate the sudden silence from the

second deputy. With Deputy Taylor, she could
understand the lack of a follow up given that he had
visited the farm on a whim, but the second deputy visit
had to be official. Something had brought him here.

But if God really is on his side —
STOP!

It just wasn't possible. Hell, she didn't even fully
believe in God. Sure, she went to church with her family
during the holidays and identified as a Christian, but deep
down inside she felt it was all bullshit.

Divine intervention wasn't at work here; Jonathan was
just getting incredibly lucky. Hopefully it wouldn't last.
Hopefully the next time someone (or a group) came to the
farm they would put an end to this ordeal.

Upstairs a floorboard creaked.

She shifted herself, a wince as she bumped her broken
hand on the ground appearing.

What was he doing now?

A few minutes earlier, after putting her down here, she
had heard his footsteps heading toward what she pictured
to be the front of the house, followed by the closing of a
door. These new steps were on the opposite side of the
house and moving much slower than his earlier ones had.

He's looking for something.
But what?

Whether or not she was actually correct on this theory
was unknown, but it seemed to fit. And given everything
that had unfolded within the kitchen she could easily see
him having dropped something that he needed.

Thoughts on what the object could be, if there even was
an object, faded as the floorboard creaks ceased. Nothing
else followed. No sounds of him walking back, no sounds
of deputies arriving, nothing.

Don't just sit here!

Do something!
She didn't.
She couldn't.

Nothing physical was standing in her way, not her broken wrist, not the jagged piece of bullet fragment (or lock fragment?) that had dug into her side, not the overall pain from being beaten on twice by Jonathan. It was mental and she knew it. All her attempts had failed and honestly, she couldn't think of anything that would succeed down here. The door would be locked. Why else would he choose this location for her? And any object she could use as a weapon would fail. Her broken hand would make sure of that given that it was linked to the hand she would use to try to fight him.

But maybe you could get lucky, a part of her mind urged.

As true as this possibility was, she still didn't make a move toward exploring the area. Instead, she simply stayed in the corner, back against the wall, broken hand cradled in her lap, teeth clenched against the constant pain, mind wishing she had never decided upon this stupid scarecrow subject matter.

* * *

She didn't exactly lose consciousness, but she wasn't fully conscious either, her mind seemingly shutting itself down for a period of time as she sat there, almost as if it had entered a meditative state.

And then the floorboard creaked again, somewhere near the front door.

Questions on what he was doing appeared once again, the possible answers coming and going without much thought. Not that it mattered at this point. She was stuck and there wasn't anything she could do about it. All her escape attempts had failed. She needed rescue not escape. It was that simple. It was –

She had no idea how much time had passed between the floorboard creak and the sudden eruption of gunfire. All she knew was that she jumped when it started and was breathing heavily when it ended a few seconds later.

A series of hurried footsteps followed, their destination being the top of the cellar stairs, light appearing on the floor beneath them as the door was thrown open.

Someone was here!

And they had had a gun!

But who had come out on top?

Who was coming down the stairs?

The answer arrived as he stepped into the light, an answer that should have been clear from the start given the lack of hesitation in running to her location. Jonathan was the only one that knew she was down here, and now his appearance in the light and his shouts at her to get up and come with him, proved him the victor in the brief shootout. Once again, luck had been on his side. It was too much to bear.

She did not stand on his command, which forced him to come to her and yank her to her feet. The pain this caused in her broken hand was nearly enough to knock her into that unconscious state she craved. The fall as she was hurried up the steps was another near miss, the consciousness clinging to her for some reason.

Scott

The first bullet hit him in the hip and the second tore through his left hand, both shots landing before he even had a chance to pull his own trigger. Once he did, the boy was already twisting away from view, the three rounds Scott fired missing him completely.

"Fuck!" he shouted while sinking down upon the stairs, pain arriving as the surge of adrenaline faded. It felt like someone had taken a hammer to his hipbone.

He then took a look at his hand, eyes startled to see that only three fingers and a thumb were there.

No more ring finger, his mind noted, the inner voice solemn.

Movement!

Down below the gun appeared once again and blindly fired two more shot, one of which whizzed right by his ear, his hair feeling a twitch as if it had been brushed.

He fired a round himself, trying to hit the hand before it disappeared, but missing by at least three feet.

After that he managed to scoot himself up the remaining steps amid the pain, and got onto the landing, his own gun hand the only thing that would be visible should the boy try to shoot him again.

Nothing.

Scott waited.

"Get up!" a voice echoed from somewhere down below.

A few screams followed, ones that he knew belonged to Holly.

She's alive!

And she's down there!

Heart racing, Scott started down the steps, hip protesting the shift he made in order to hobble from one to the next, but failing to prevent his decent.

While managing this he heard several more cries from Holly, his anger and hatred toward the boy rising. He wanted to kill him. And the family wherever the fuck they were. One shot for each, bullet between the eyes, brain splattering out upon whatever surface was present. Such an act wouldn't just be for him and Holly, but for humanity as well. People like this had no place within the world. Their deaths were totally justified.

A spent shell casing caught his foot on the third step, his eyes having failed to see it given his focus on the area beyond the stairs where the boy might reappear.

Pain erupted as his hip twisted, the sheer agony knocking away all control and bringing forth a scream.

"Scott!" Holly cried.

The voice somehow eased his mind despite the terror that was present.

"Holly!" he shouted back as his body finished its crumble down the last two steps, the pain unlike anything he had ever felt before. "Over here!"

He heard a commotion followed by a cry from the boy.

"Fucker!" Holly shouted and then screamed, the sound horrific.

Hearing this, Scott pushed himself off the floor with his wounded hand, a moment of regret arriving with its use, and then crashed into the front door as his hip refused to accept his own weight.

Nothing more than a heavy grunt was released,

followed by the sound of his teeth grinding together as the pain eased off a bit.

A crash from the kitchen erupted, as did more shouts and then several gunshots.

Silence.

Panicked, Scott moved toward the kitchen, body using the wall as a crutch, gun ready, fear of what he would find causing horrific images to appear within his mind.

Another crash and suddenly the scuffle within continued, the sound of something heavy – probably a pot – slamming into the floor.

He was almost there.

Glass shattered, followed by an odd whoosh and then a scream that stopped him in his tracks, the horror it contained almost too much to comprehend.

Holly gasped.

Burnt flesh!

Something was on fire.

A door slammed.

Smoke appeared.

And then Holly was in the hallway, coming at him, feet unsteady yet somehow maintaining balance.

Her eyes went wide when she saw him, as did his own.

"Holly!" he cried.

She came at him, but then screamed as her hands crashed into his chest, his mind having expected her arms to spread as she embraced him as his own had done.

His hip then gave out as he tried to steady her and the two fell to the floor, her knee slamming into the wound and bringing a burst of yellow sparks to his mind.

Somehow, he managed to hold onto his consciousness.

The same could not be said about Holly, though he wasn't exactly sure what led to it given that she hadn't hit her head, her fall broken by her hands.

Smoke began to spread along the hallway ceiling.

"Holly," he said, shaking her. "Holly, get up."

She said something that he wasn't able to identify, eyes still closed, body limp.

"Holly!"

Thicker plumes of smoke flowed from the doorway, as did a sudden increase in temperature. The fire was spreading.

He had no choice. He shifted Holly around so that he could get some room to move and slapped her across the face while shouting at her to wake up.

It worked. Her eyes sprang open and focused on him, a confused glare forming until she realized the situation. Panic appeared. And then she started coughing as her lungs tasted the smoke in the air.

"Come on, we have to get out of here," Scott said, a siren suddenly appearing somewhere outside. "Can you stand?"

Holly nodded.

Though it seemed doubtful anyone could be in the kitchen given the sheer volume of smoke and heat that was now pouring from it, Scott kept his gun trained on the doorway as he struggled to his feet, finger touching the trigger and ready to squeeze should anyone appear.

Once up, Holly attempted to help him balance, but could do very little with her arms linked together. The hunched stance they had to take due to the smoke above also made this awkward, so he urged her to just get herself out the front door.

She shook her head and stayed at his side, though whether this was out of concern for him or due to her own fear that the family would be out there waiting was unknown.

Outside the siren continued to build and then came the

sound of tires skidding on gravel.

Fear that the deputy would be shot as he stepped out of the car arrived.

Does he even have the gun still?

If not, other family members might.

But where were they?

He tried asking about this, but the smoke was too much and hit the back of his throat before any words could be formed. A series of coughs followed, the sudden lack of air making it nearly impossible to stay upright as they reached the door.

And then they were out on the porch, lungs heaving as they tried to suck in fresh air while expelling whatever bits of smoke tainted air had been sucked in, irritated eyes dripping tears and blurring everything.

"Drop the gun!"

Scott twisted toward the voice, a warning about the boy and family starting to leave his lips just as something struck him in the chest.

"No!" Holly screamed

Her cry reached one ear while the gunshot reached the other, a random thought on how one never hears the shot that hits them entering his mind.

His legs disappeared.

He then felt himself being dragged across the gravel, all while Holly was screaming at someone, the words not making any sense.

He was unable to breathe, his throat filling with something that caused him to gag all while the right side of his chest felt as if it were sinking. Not long after that, darkness began to edge into his vision, along with Holly who was looking down at him.

As before, he couldn't make out her words, a mute button having been pushed with his mind, but after a second, he thought he could read the words "love" and "you" leaving her lips.

"I love you too," he said, though whether the sound was vocalized for real or just in his head was a mystery.

Darkness.

Jonathan

He made it about halfway across the field before crumbling to the ground, the pain from the burns making it impossible to continue onward. Later, once he was rested, things would be better and he would be able to figure out where to go and what to do, but now he just needed to lie down and let his body settle.

Several hours passed before he was conscious again, his mind having drifted through an odd series of images and scenes, some feeling as if they were unfolding for real right alongside him. Naomi had been present in one, a fear of being left alone overwhelming her as she knelt by his side.

Does she know I'm leaving?
Is that why she came to me?
What does that mean?

Fear on what her spiritual presence on the farm could indicate about his future destination appeared. If not in Hell, did that mean such a place didn't exist, and, if so, did the same hold true of Heaven? Or had her sins not really earned her a spot in Hell like his parents had insisted, yet still been enough to keep her from entering Heaven? Was there a middle level?

He pushed himself up into a sitting position while thinking this, the burned areas on his chest and upper arm not happy with the movement. Sweat was adding to the torment as the pain returned, his body completely soaked in it despite how cool the air around him was.

You have a fever.

This thought earned no questions or debate, just a follow-up realization that he needed water, both to quench his growing thirst and to clean out the wounds he had suffered that afternoon.

You can't go back.

Or could he?

Deputies had been arriving as he ran into the corn, the flames that Holly had inflicted upon him with the stove and bacon grease having been short lived once he fell down the kitchen steps into the dirt. Whether or not they were still there after all this time was unknown, but given the lack of sounds, he didn't think this was the case. Then again, he had walked a long way before collapsing, so maybe they were still there.

And looking for you! his mind shouted.

Holly would have told them all about him, her story backed up by the young man if he had survived the gunshots . . .

He did and called out to Holly as you dragged her through the kitchen.

With this memory came the one of her sudden resistance, the attempt to grab the gun resulting in every round being fired into the wall. After that, they had crashed into the stove, the empty pot he had boiled water in earlier knocked to the ground and the burners firing up as their bodies twisted the knobs in their struggle.

And then the fire.

He had watched it leap at him as the jar of bacon grease fell from the shelf and shattered upon the stove; the sudden burst of flame seemingly directed his way while completely ignoring Holly, though maybe she had been burned as well. He didn't know. His ability to process things had ended the moment the flaming grease had splattered his chest and arm, his only goal being to get away from the flames. Of course, running while on fire wasn't a good idea, but the realization that he actually had caught didn't arrive until after it had been put out, his tripping down the steps outside the kitchen door and landing in the dirt having smothered them. It was then that he realized the deputies were arriving and fled.

* * *

Darkness began to overwhelm the field as he made his way back toward the house, concern over the smoke he saw rising up –- along with a burning smell different from that of his own cooked flesh -- pushing away the other concern that deputies would be there waiting for him. In fact, the closer he got, the greater the first concern became while the second one grew less and less, the lack of sounds from the area making it pretty obvious that the place was deserted. Even so, he still moved cautiously through the corn, his hope being he would make it close enough to see what the situation was before the light completely faded.

* * *

The house was gone, the chimney and a few charred first level walls being the only thing that still stood. The rest had caved into itself and burned, his body able to feel the heat drifting from it while on the edge of the field.

No deputies were present.

He was alone.

Sadness started to arrive, but couldn't get a full grip on him as his need for water was his main focus at the moment.

Would the pipes still work?

If not, he would have to use the pump by the well, which didn't appeal to him, not with the movement that would be required to actually bring the water up. A short attempt at trying to explore the smoldering ruins for the pipes that would have led to the kitchen sink proved how foolish such a task was, the rubble simply too hot for him to do an adequate search.

And if even one pipe had been opened, no water would come, his mind said, though he wondered how accurate this truly was.

As feared, working the handle on the well pump was excruciating, the cooked flesh on his chest cracking open after the first few pumps, and by the time water started to flow he could feel blood leaking from several areas.

It was worth it though, the water soothing his throat and, once he got a bucket and rag from within the barn, feeling great against his burns.

* * *

You can't stay here, he told himself ten minutes later while eyeing the barn and visualizing his body crawling atop one of the piles of straw in the loft with a wool blanket. *Just because they aren't here now doesn't mean they won't return in the morning.*

And they will be searching for you.

You have to leave.

Once again, questions on where he could go and what he would do appeared in his mind, the lack of answers weighing him down. Adding to the problem was his inability to start the truck, the keys somewhere within the smoldering pile of rubble.

You still have the chief's keys.

They were in his pocket, the pointed edge making itself known as he leaned against the barn.

Such a long walk, a weary part of his mind said, the idea of simply finding a place to sleep within the barn gaining appeal.

You can't stay here, he repeated to himself. *And the sooner you start walking the sooner you will make it to the car.*

Will I even be able to get it out of the weeds?

Earlier he had really worked the car into the overgrowth, his hope being that it would be invisible from the road. And now he needed it.

Only one way to find out.

He started walking, body moving slow due to the burns and exhaustion, feet catching everything that crossed his path given how little he actually lifted them.

Can't make it, his mind decided. It was just too much to walk across the entire field.

Should have just gone to the car in the beginning.

No, he had needed to see the house. He had needed to see what had happened after he fled. He had –

His eyes caught sight of the scarecrow post, the path he was walking bringing him fairly close to its location.

It's gone!

Or is it?

It was hard to tell in the growing darkness, the shadows making it impossible to see for certain.

Go! Run!

No, he had to be sure. He had to know if the scarecrow had broken free or if it was simply slumped in such a way that allowed the shadows to hide it.

If it is free . . .

Memories of that horrible night all those years ago played out in his mind, first with the screaming from Naomi as the two were caught, and then the screaming from the boyfriend as they put his struggling form upon the post, his father's suggestion of using nails to keep him in place being vetoed by his grandfather for fear that it would somehow mock the crucifixion of their Lord and Savoir.

Would nails of held it down better? Jonathan now wondered while moving closer, body demanding he stop and just rest for a while. *Or would it have still broken free and tried to kill us all in our sleep?*

The answer to this depended upon whether or not this new scarecrow had broken free of the chains, because if it was able to do that then that would mean the one before would probably have been able to break free of nails as well, the strength one acquired when becoming a scarecrow seemingly limitless.

Yet vulnerable to a shotgun?

Again, confusion on this plagued him, his mind unable to truly grasp the details of how and why of the scarecrows. The only thing he knew was that they were evil and, once created, would do whatever they could to destroy the virtue and salvation of the family.

Feet heavy with exhaustion, and body slowed by pain, he stepped from the cornstalks into the small scarecrow clearing, eyes confirming what he had feared. The scarecrow was gone, the chains crumbled at the base of the post where they had fallen.

Fearing an attack, he spun around to see if the scarecrow had been lying in wait.

Nothing but dark withered cornstalks met his eyes. Even the chief's body was gone.

It wouldn't wait here once down . . .

No, it would have come for him. In fact, it had probably been near where he had passed out earlier, its journey toward him slowed by the missing foot.

And now it will be coming toward this location, its bloodlust boiling over . . .

GO!

He turned to flee, his goal being to get to the chief's car and drive as far away as possible.

He made it three steps, his foot recognizing the trigger mechanism of the trap seconds before the pain of the teeth snapping into his leg appeared.

Screams echoed across the field, ones that he didn't recognize as his own at first, his only focus being to pull his leg free, hands struggling to pry the rusty teeth from within his shin.

It was no use.

The pain was too much and his fear too overwhelming.

He couldn't get free.

He . . .

Naomi was standing over him, a look of sadness upon her face.

Words of comfort followed, though whether they were real, or just something he imagined he couldn't tell. Everything seemed fuzzy as if the world were slipping away. Even the pain was fading, his body feeling somehow cushioned and soothed.

Monday, September 16, 2012

Holly

She spent most of the night bouncing from one horrific dream to the next, the visions within her head so realistic, and her mind so certain that each was a current reality, that she now wondered if the dreams had actually been med-fueled hallucinations. The current state of exhaustion added to this theory, her thinking being there was no way she could have been asleep that entire time and still be tired.

But maybe it wasn't enough?

Maybe you'll be tired for several days?

Maybe –

A nurse walked in to check on her followed by an orderly with a breakfast tray. Seeing the food brought up several images of Jonathan bringing her breakfast, the only difference here being the plastic cup of coffee and packets of cream and sugar. Actually, the taste was a big difference as well, the food Jonathan had made so much better than what they had brought. Not that she would wish a switch in situations. The lack of quality when compared to Jonathan's cooking also didn't prevent her from finishing everything on the tray, her hunger seeming to grow with each bite until nothing but a few crumbles of cold rubbery egg remained.

"Looks like someone *was* hungry," the nurse said while coming back in a few minutes later, an announcement that an investigator with the county was there to speak with her once more the reason for the visit.

"I don't want to talk to them," Holly muttered. She pushed the tray table away from the bed and crossed her arms.

"Oh sweetie, I don't think you really have a choice in that." She checked something with the IV. "Besides, you want them to catch the guy who broke your hand, don't you?"

Holly didn't reply, the implication that the damage to her hand was the defining example of the injuries she had sustained while in captivity causing her anger to flair. Seeing the investigator who walked in a few seconds later added fuel, her mind unable to separate him from the deputy who had shot Scott.

* * *

"We found the body this morning near the post where your boyfriend had been hung up," the investigator started. "We suspect it is the young man who held you prisoner at the farm given the burns and because he was in possession of the former chief's keys and cell phone, but don't yet have a positive ID on him."

"His name is Jonathan," Holly said. "Turner. Jonathan Turner."

"Yes," the investigator said with a nod. "You gave us the name last night. Unfortunately, we have no record of such a person existing, and, since you said he was living there alone, we have no way of confirming this without your visual identification."

"Oh."

"We also have no way of knowing how old he was. Did he mention his age at all, or what exactly happened with his family?"

Holly shook her head. "He didn't say much, just that

his parents had died in a car crash and that his sister had
been a sinner – born in sin, actually, whatever that
means."

The investigator nodded and then waited for more.
When nothing else was said, he asked, "That all?"

She shrugged. "He kept me chained in the loft of the
barn for two weeks and really only came up there to bring
me food and clean out the bedpan." *Not exactly fertile
ground for deep and meaningful conversations.*

"Still, even the smallest thing could be helpful,
something you overheard him mutter, or a statement that
might help connect the other things you heard."

"No, nothing."

"Are you sure," he continued. "It's really important."

This time she didn't bother with a reply and simply
stared at him.

He waited.

She crossed her arms; face wincing as the IV was
snagged by the bedrail, and then said, "I really can't help
you."

"Okay." He stood, hands pocketing the notebook. "If
you're feeling up to it, I'll have a nurse get a wheelchair so
we can go identify the body."

Holly didn't reply.

"Are you feeling up to it?"

Holly sighed. "I guess."

"Great. I'll go get the nurse."

"I can walk." With that, she shifted herself to the edge
of the bed and attempted to stand. It was a huge mistake.

* * *

"Coyotes got to him at some point this morning, but the
face was left pretty much untouched," the investigator
said while she was being wheeled down, the near fall
while getting out of bed having changed her opinion on

using a wheelchair. "They've been pretty bad in this area lately due to the drought."

Nothing else followed, Holly's lack of reply to the pointless rambling having silenced him.

Not long after that, the nurse was taking her back to her room, an odd statement on how it must have been difficult to see a dead body leaving her lips. Again, Holly didn't reply and would have stayed silent for the trip back if not for the sudden desire to see Scott.

"Oh, honey, he's still in the ICU," the nurse said. "Seeing him like that wouldn't be much fun."

"But he is he allowed visitors, right?"

"Yes, but -- "

"Then I want to see him."

* * *

Scott's bed looked like a tangled mess of wires and tubes that had been set atop a body, one that didn't look alive. Alive he was, however, the steady beep from the machine evidence of this.

"They'll keep him in the coma for a few days while the lung heals, and then move him into a regular room for the duration of his stay," the ICU nurse said.

Holly nodded, eyes threatening tears, a question on exactly how long that process would be going unasked.

A minute and then two passed.

"Is it okay if I stay with him a while?" she asked, head nodding toward a chair tucked into the back of the room behind the machines.

"Are you family?"

"Girlfriend," Holly said.

"Um . . ." the nurse considered this and then, with a nod, said, "Yeah, go ahead."

"Thanks."

An hour later, when her parents finally arrived, they

found her sitting by Scott's side, the room chair having been repositioned so she could face him while also holding his hand. It was an unexpected sight for them, one that they chose not to disturb.

About the Author

William Malmborg has been publishing short stories in horror magazines and dark fiction anthologies since 2002. In addition to **DARK HARVEST**, three of his novels, **JIMMY**, **NIKKI'S SECRET** and **TEXT MESSAGE**, are available, as is a short story collection titled **SCRAPING THE BONE** that features five previously published and five original tales of horror.

To learn more about William Malmborg check out his webpage at:

http://www.williammalmborg.com/

You can also friend him on Facebook at:

http://www.facebook.com/wlmalmborg